I0730092

RUN, RUN, RUN

JAY MCALISTER

Copyright © Jay McAlister 2025

Written by Jay McAlister and Karli Florisson

First published by Hembury Books in 2025

hemburybooks.com.au

info@hemburybooks.com

ISBN 9781764055222 (ebook)

ISBN 9781764055215 (paperback)

ISBN 9781764055239 (hardback)

The moral right of the author has been asserted.

All rights reserved. No portion of this book may be reproduced in any form without permission from the author and publisher, except as permitted by Australian copyright law.

A catalogue record for this book is available from the National Library of Australia

For JJ and Imo x

ABOUT THE AUTHOR

The oldest child in a big, busy family, Jay McAlister grew up in Woodridge, and later on the Sunshine Coast. He worked a range of jobs, everything from surf instructing to pumping petrol, eventually becoming a carpenter by trade.

He bought his first property at 19, beating his former maths teacher in the auction. Since then, Jay has started and run various successful businesses, working in advertising, construction, a record label, TV and more. Despite being semi-retired, Jay now finds himself busier than ever between business interests and making time for creative pursuits.

Jay still lives on the Sunshine Coast, where he enjoys playing the guitar, cooking for friends and family, singing loudly and dancing at any opportunity he can get. His two children mean the world to him.

Inspired by some of his own life experiences, *Run, Run, Run* is Jay's first book. He plans to keep writing, making music, coming up with new ideas and living his life with exuberance and enthusiasm.

hemburybooks.com.au/jay-mcalister

CONTENTS

Chapter 1	1
Chapter 2	9
Chapter 3	17
Chapter 4	25
Chapter 5	35
Chapter 6	43
Chapter 7	53
Chapter 8	61
Chapter 9	71
Chapter 10	79
Chapter 11	85
Chapter 12	93
Chapter 13	101
Chapter 14	109
Chapter 15	117
Chapter 16	123
Chapter 17	129
Chapter 18	137
Chapter 19	143
Chapter 20	149
Chapter 21	155
Chapter 22	163
Epilogue	167

CHAPTER 1

The night started out just like any other. They'd done this a hundred times before, maybe more. Any opportunity to celebrate was a good one, and tonight it was Mitch's birthday. Tommo was celebrating a promotion at work, and Jason was adding to the general merriment by celebrating the fact his construction project was ahead of schedule. The table was stacked with empty beer glasses, plates, picked-over salads and a few food scraps. In front of Mitch was a half-eaten cupcake with a birthday candle in it, but otherwise, not many leftovers from this group.

Jason glanced around at his friends. There were fewer of them these days. Back in their post-high school days, there would have been more than twenty of them on a night out. There were the usual guys – friends since primary school – and an assortment of girlfriends as well as other friends who came and went. The numbers had dropped off over the years, thinned out by interstate moves and the commitments of families and kids. But tonight there were eight of them, which was a good turnout for a Friday night.

Jason sat back in his chair, watching as the guys drained the last of their beers. They were at a seafood restaurant in Golden Sands with a view of the beach. The food had been great, but already some of the guys were starting to look at their phones and make noises about heading home. They all ribbed each other about getting soft. Back when they were younger, their nights out wouldn't start until ten or eleven o'clock, but Tommo's kids had soccer early in the morning, and Gaz's wife was on his case about getting home to finish some home renovation he'd been working on for weeks.

Things like that made Jason glad to be single and free as a bird, his kids nearly grown and independent these days. Plus, it meant he could wink at the pretty blonde waitress without feeling a shred of guilt as she cleared away their plates. Maybe later he'd stop to chat with her., see if he could get her phone number. Or maybe not. There were plenty of beautiful women on the Sunshine Coast, and Jason had all the time in the world.

He said goodbye as the guys filed out with the usual promises to catch up for a barbeque soon. Still, he felt a bittersweet pang when he thought of their early days, when at this time of night, they'd all be onto their fifth beer, or tenth, maybe, raring to go out to drink and dance and see what adventures the night held. He missed those days. Still, life was pretty great now too, so he couldn't complain.

'Looks like it's just us, JMac,' Pauly said, draining the last of his beer. 'I hope all those fuckers have paid their bills and not left it to us.'

Jason laughed. 'All good, I've got it anyway.'

'Yeah, yeah, we all know you're a big shot businessman these days.'

'Right. You're not exactly on the bones of your arse either, Pauly.'

The conversation carried on, with the good-natured mocking that was the shorthand for their friendship. Around them, the waitstaff were clearing the dishes from the tables. Jason wanted another drink, but felt the now-familiar hesitation. There'd been too many nights in his past when one more had turned into drinking until he was out of control, past the point of black-outs and bad decisions. Too many times, he'd woken to the bitter taste of regret in his mouth.

He still drank on social occasions, but these days he knew his limits. Or maybe he was kidding himself. Either way, he didn't follow the siren call of alcohol as blindly as he had in the past. Maybe it was a sign he was growing up. Getting old. He smiled to himself. Fuck getting old. He was planning to stay young as long as he could.

'So, what do you reckon?' Pauly asked. 'Want to kick on? There's got to be a pub with some live music around here somewhere.'

'Don't you have to get home to Sharon and the kids?'

'Nah. They're off visiting her sister in Noosa. I'm on my own for the weekend.'

'Then let's go. I've been wanting to see what it's like around here at night.'

Golden Sands was an up-and-coming area with lots of new development in progress. One of the projects that was set to transform the area was Jason's new development, an apartment complex with a set of shops on the ground floor. Everything was going to plan, which was so unusual on a construction site it made Jason feel prickly with anticipation. Something was bound to go wrong at any moment. Still, for the time being, everything was great and he felt like celebrating. Not that that was unusual – Jason was always the first on the dance floor and the last to go home from every party. And tonight, he was eager to see what Golden Sands had to offer.

The beachfront strip of restaurants and pubs was humming with tourists and locals. The night was still and warm, and people were walking in groups, laughing and talking. Jason watched the tourists with their peeling sunburn and happy faces, the teenagers eager for excitement and the young lovers walking hand in hand. There was the hum of excitement in the air, mingling with the salty air of the beach, where the waves lapped gently at the sand and the water glimmered in the moonlight.

He and Pauly walked through the throngs of people until they found a pub with a band they knew. The band was called Peach Fur and, as always, their music was a riot of grungy guitar and great riffs. They listened for a while and bought drinks for a couple of gorgeous, sparkly-eyed women standing at the bar. The band took a break and he and Pauly said hi to the young musicians as they downed a beer between sets. But, as the band headed back onto the stage and started up again with a mellow number, Jason began itching for something you could dance to. He caught Pauly's eye and motioned toward the door.

'Let's go somewhere else.'

Pauly was deep in conversation with the woman they'd met at the bar, but he had the same kind of restless intensity as Jason. He nodded, made his excuses to the woman, and gave her a wink as he headed for the door. Outside, the sidewalks were still busy with well-dressed young people, all out looking for adventure.

'Where do you want to go?' Pauly stifled a yawn. 'I need another drink, it's past my bedtime already.'

Jason laughed. 'Shit, you're getting old, man. Come on. Back in the day, we'd just be gathering steam by now.'

Most of those nights blended together in his mind, but what stood out was the sense of possibility that anything could happen. He could meet the love of his life, or come up with the perfect business idea, or stumble into enlightenment on the beach, watching the stars with someone he'd just met. He missed that sense of wide-open horizons. His life had turned out great, even better than he had imagined, but there was something about the endless optimism of youth he missed. He didn't miss the raging hangovers and being broke half the time, though.

'Hey, I know. There's a club next door to my build site that I've been wanting to check out. It's called Galaxy, I think.'

'Let's go.'

They fell back into old patterns easily, Jason thinking up plans and making wild suggestions, Pauly always up for whatever he wanted to do. They walked through the streets, dodging drunk people and groups of partygoers. The wafting smell of food filled the night air, plus the occasional stink of piss as they walked past an alley. The build site was a few streets back from the beach, surrounded by coffee shops and offices. The apartments would have a great view of Golden Sands Beach, and the shops below would fit right into the bustling centre of the suburb, which was rapidly changing from a sleepy little patch of suburbia into a tourist hotspot. It was a great location.

They walked until they could see the shell of the complex rising from the security fences below and the scaffolding that surrounded it. Jason felt a sense of pride. Golden Sands had been a bit of a backwater along the bustling Sunshine Coast when he'd bought the block of land.

Now it was one of the up-and-coming areas, full of new restaurants and hotels, with more development projects dotted around the centre.

Just down the street from the build site was a square structure, painted a deep blue. In daylight it looked a bit run down, with peeling paint and rusted security bars over the windows. At night, the front of the building was lit up with floodlights and you could see the speckles of stars painted across its façade. A sign proclaimed Galaxy Nightclub in a bold font.

As they got closer, Jason could hear the muffled thud of bass-heavy music echoing from inside. There wasn't a queue and the bouncer waved them in with a bored stare. Not a great sign. Inside, it took a moment for Jason's eyes to adjust to the darkness and the flashing lights, but the music immediately took him back to the many nights he'd spent on the dance floor in past years. It felt like a second home.

'Let's get a drink,' Pauly shouted over the music. In the strobing lights they could see that the big room was half empty. There were a few groups of people on the dance floor and some more standing around the bar. For a Friday night, it was a small crowd, thought Jason. Maybe they were too early and the crowd was still building up. He followed his mate over to the bar and downed the drink Pauly had ordered in a couple of gulps. It was a Scotch and Dry, and it took him straight back to his younger years.

'Come on, man, let's hit the dance floor,' he said. But Pauly was still nursing his drink, so they stood by the bar instead. From the dim corner, they watched the groups of people milling around them. There was a cluster of women who were obviously at a hen's party, some of them wearing sashes that pronounced *bride* or *bridesmaid*. The bride-to-be was staggering, laughing hysterically at some joke through her white veil. Jason smiled, thinking that she'd be feeling sorry for herself in the morning.

He watched a group of skinny young men with gelled hair trying to impress a couple of bored-looking blonde girls in skin-tight dresses and sky-high heels. Behind the bar, some of the bartenders were leaning against the back wall, chatting to each other while they waited for customers. A hint of stale beer lingered in the air. His earlier enthusiasm for this place was wearing off. The Galaxy had rather a sad air about it, as if it was past its prime. It felt a bit seedy. Maybe he was too sober, and this was what nightclubs felt like when you weren't roaring drunk. He thought about it. No, he'd been fairly sober on plenty of their nights out, dancing like a demon instead. It was just this place. There was something about it that gave him the creeps.

Pauly started talking to a woman standing next to him at the bar but Jason wasn't in the mood. He wanted to people-watch instead. He smiled at the scenes he saw around him. By now, the bride in the bachelorette group was crying, sobbing onto her bridesmaid's shoulders. The gel-haired men were breaking out their dance moves but the two blonde girls weren't interested; their eyes only for each other.

A sudden movement along the dark wall caught his eye. A young woman hurried along in the shadows, in the direction of the front door. Jason watched her. She looked furtive, like a mouse trying to stay out of sight. There was a rush behind her and a tall man dressed in black grabbed her arm and pulled her around to face him. Jason could sense the tension in the air between them. The woman, who reminded him somehow of his own daughter, pulled back, cowering away from the man. Immediately all of Jason's protective instincts kicked in and he stood, taking a few steps toward the scene that way playing out in front of him.

The tall man, wearing a black bomber jacket and black jeans, leaned in to the woman, saying something Jason couldn't hear. But he could easily interpret the body language. The man was threatening her. Jason wasn't a fighter, but he wasn't about to let this slide either. He abhorred men who abused women, or anyone weaker than themselves, really. He could see the girl was afraid. The man lifted his hand in a gesture that was clearly a threat to hit her. Jason was already striding across the room toward them. In two steps he reached the girl. He grabbed the man's raised arm and growled, 'Don't you even think about hitting her.'

Up close, he could see the man was young and skinny, his acne-blemished face creased with an ugly scowl at Jason's interference. His pupils were dilated and his jaw clenched and unclenched. He was clearly on something. His eyes flickered over Jason, taking in his height, his rugby player's shoulders and the muscles bunching in his forearm as he tightened his fist. Reluctantly, the younger man took a step backward.

'This is none of your business. Fuck off,' he said to Jason, spitting with emotion, his eyes full of venom.

Jason ignored him and turned to the girl. She was still cowering beside him. Up close, he could see how young she was. Barely older than his own daughter. She had black hair styled in a blunt bob and eyes that seemed too big for her pale face.

'You okay?' he asked. The girl stared at him and nodded. 'This guy bothering you?' She lowered her eyes and didn't reply.

'Look man, I told you to fuck off,' the skinny guy said. Jason glanced over to the front door. The bored-looking bouncer hadn't noticed them.

'Come on, Stella, come with me,' the skinny guy said, grabbing the girl by the wrist and pulling her toward him. She let out a little cry that Jason could hear over the pulsing music.

'Leave her alone,' Jason said, his voice filled with steel.

The young man, eyes wide and jaw working back and forward, let go of the girl's arm and lunged. Jason easily dodged the punch. One of the benefits of growing up with brothers who were always play-fighting and wrestling was that it gave you sharp reflexes. Always prepared for an attack. Jason laughed. He could feel a jolt of adrenaline in his veins. But the young man was serious, squaring up for a fight. The girl cowered away from the violence. Seeing her fear made some bit of self-control snap inside of Jason. He stepped forward and swung his fist at the other guy's face, putting all of his weight behind it.

His fist hit his target, and he felt the guy's cheekbone hard against his knuckles. He followed the momentum with his second fist, which hit the other side of the guy's face, jolting his head backward. For a moment, he could see shock in the young man's eyes, and then he fell backward onto the floor. He lay stunned for a few seconds, and then scrambled away from Jason, letting out a string of profanities. He got to his feet and made a beeline for an unmarked door. Jason presumed it led to a back room, maybe some kind of rear exit. He let him go. He figured the guy would be nursing a black eye and a bruised face that might teach him a few manners. He turned toward the girl.

'Are you okay?'

She was staring at him like a deer caught in the headlights. 'Yeah. Yes, I'm fine. Thank you.' Her voice was raspy and barely audible over the music. She pushed her hair back from her face. Jason could see her hands were trembling.

'You want me to get you a taxi or something? Do you have some friends who can help you get home?'

She shook her head. 'No. I'm fine, I… I live nearby.'

From the corner of his eye, Jason could see a solidly built man dressed in a black suit coming from the doorway where the skinny guy had fled. Jason smiled. Looks like the kid had some kind of connection to the Galaxy's management, and he'd been off telling tales. He looked at the girl again. There was something in her pale, frightened face that made him think she needed a friend. Jason reached into his pocket and pulled out a business card. 'Well, if you ever need any help, or have any more problems with that creep, call me, okay? My name's Jason. And you're Stella, is that right?'

She nodded and took the card, slipping it into her pocket without looking at it. 'Thank you.' Then she turned and walked quickly toward the front door.

As Jason had guessed, the big goon walked over and stood in front of him, arms folded across his chest. 'You need to leave.' His voice sounded like the rasp of gravel on concrete.

Jason checked to see if the girl had made it safely out the door. She'd vanished from sight. 'Yeah, yeah. I'm going.'

As long as the girl was safe, he wasn't planning to pick any more fights. He went to find Pauly, suddenly feeling too old and far too sober for this place. Plus, he had to be at the building site early the next morning. He looked around the club one more time. He couldn't wait to get out of the place. Something didn't feel right about the Galaxy.

CHAPTER 2

On a building site, Jason expected delays. He expected supply issues, late tradies, unforeseen problems. But he didn't expect this kind of thing. Shit, he didn't even understand what the hell was going on. Maybe going out last night to celebrate how well everything was going had jinxed things on the site.

It had all been going smoothly until he arrived on site that morning to see a trail of destruction. He stood in the middle of the complex his company was building and looked around. The concrete floor was covered with detritus. Pipes that had been laid by the plumbers the day before were now splintered and broken. Some of the electrical wiring had been pulled out of the wall. More plumbing supplies, which yesterday had been stacked neatly beside the wall, lay strewn across the floor. A porcelain sink, ready to install in one of the ground-floor bathrooms, was shattered into large chunks. There were cracks in some wall frameworks that looked like someone had taken a sledge-hammer to it. And smeared along one cement wall, in dripping red paint that looked like blood, someone had scrawled *Run run run, you can't outrun me.*

'Rachel,' Jason called. She didn't usually visit the build sites, preferring to orchestrate things behind the scenes like a conductor who coaxed flawless performances from a rag-tag group of musicians. But she'd come along to take a look at how things were progressing this morning. It was early enough that most of the workers were still getting their morning coffees and pulling on their work boots. Rachel, of course, was immaculately dressed and didn't need caffeine to be at her best. He could hear the clicking of her heels as she walked over. She was wearing a grey pantsuit with shoes he was sure cost more than his whole outfit. As per the site regulations, she had on a yellow hard hat. Beneath it, her silky grey hair framed her face. 'Yes, Jason, what's going on?'

A half-built stud wall hid the sight in the main room from her. Wordlessly, Jason waved her over and gestured at the destruction. Another person seeing such ruin might gasp or exclaim loudly. Not his chief financial officer. Rachel simply raised an eyebrow and said, 'Oh. Perhaps we'd better call the police.' She took out her mobile phone and dialled.

Jason felt a surge of irritation. The plumbers and electricians were going to have to redo this entire section, and some parts of the wall framing would need to be replaced as well. Plus, they'd need to order new materials. And who knew how long it would take the police to investigate? It was going to set him back a couple of days at least. He'd optimistically hoped this project would pull off the small miracle of finishing ahead of schedule. Perhaps not. He knew better than that.

The building site was still quiet before the usual bustle of the day got underway. He looked around. Jason had been excited about this project, but as it often did, his attention had begun to wander lately. He was already thinking about the next development, the next big thing he wanted to accomplish. He'd mentioned some of his ideas to Rachel and she'd told him in no uncertain terms that he should wait until this project was finished before he dived into the next big idea. 'Beware the octopus of opportunity, Jason,' she'd said.

It wasn't the first time she'd said something like that, and he'd smiled back at her affectionately. The problem was, there were so many exciting possibilities and he was always itching to get onto the next project. But he was smart enough to know that if Rachel gave you advice, you should listen. Still, it was hard to stop his mind from filling with ideas. He always got bored focusing on just one project at a time. There was nothing for it, though, but to knuckle down and get the complex finished. Then he could get on to the next project. And the next.

There was another reason for haste when it came to this project, though. Just two streets away another luxury apartment complex was being built. The developer was Brian Welsh, and the complex was similar enough to Jason's development that it wasn't hard to guess that Brian had copied him. The bastard. It wouldn't be the first time. They'd worked together way back when Jason was starting out in construction. Back when he was building backyard decks for a living, Brian had been on his team. A fairly lazy chippie who hated being told what to do. They were around the same age, and Brian obviously resented having to work for Jason. Even though it had been Jason's business, Jason's team, from the start, Brian always thought he knew better. That had led to some expensive mistakes, and so Jason had secretly been happy when Brian had told him he was quitting to start up his own business. Perhaps not so secretly. Jason was the kind of guy who didn't usually succeed in hiding his emotions.

Still, there'd been no hard feelings. He and Brian were mates. Well, more like rivals these days, but friendly rivals. Jason was on track to finish his apartment complex before Brian finished his, which was important. Whoever finished first would get first pick of tenants in the shops below and the buyers with the deepest pockets lining up to buy the apartments. The thought tugged at the edge of his consciousness. Maybe Brian had done this? Maybe he had underestimated just how much of a chip Brian had on his shoulder? He shook away the thoughts. Surely not.

***

The police arrived with a flurry of sirens, which Jason felt was unnecessary for a case of vandalism. He waited inside while Rachel clacked off in her Italian leather heels to show them through to where the destruction was. A police officer with a steely-eyed stare and her hair pulled back into a tight bun introduced herself as Detective Riggs.

Jason shook the hand she held out and thought about cracking a joke. He stifled a smile and told himself it wasn't the right time for humour. Plus, from the detective's glare, she didn't seem to be in possession of a sense of humour. Instead, he showed Detective Riggs the damage to the building site and answered her questions. Her offsider, a tall officer with a crooked nose and a slightly rumpled uniform, wandered around taking photos of the mess.

By this time, a small crowd of curious tradies and chippies had gathered, all in their hi-vis and at least half of them sipping Cokes or iced coffees. Detective Riggs nodded her head toward the assembled group. 'We'll need to talk to anyone who was on site early this morning, just in case they might have seen something. Who's got access to the site?'

Jason laughed. 'A lot of people.' He thought of the many hands it took to build a complex like this, everyone from architects to concreters to apprentices. 'I was first on site this morning, so I unlocked the gates. But normally, Frank would do that. He's the foreman.'

Jason waved Frank over from the group of gawking spectators. He introduced him to the detective. 'Frank has a list of everyone who's got access to the site. He can take it from here.'

Frank had worked for him for years, and even though he had a reputation for being short-tempered and cranky, he was a great builder. Frank was wearing paint-splattered work gear, steel-capped Blundstones and the prerequisite hard hat. He nodded awkwardly at Detective Riggs.

'Great. We'll need a copy of that list, please. Before you go, Jason, just a couple more questions.' Detective Riggs frowned in his direction. 'Is there anyone you can think of who might have a grudge against you? Someone who would want to damage your property?'

Jason laughed. 'No, I don't think so. I mean, I've had my little differences with people over the years, but really, I get on well with everyone. I'm a people person.' He shrugged. 'I can't think of anyone who has it in for me.'

Detective Riggs nodded and made a little note in her notepad. 'And these words.' She gestured to the red paint on the walls. 'Someone obviously took the time to paint this message on the wall, even though it could have led to them getting caught. Any idea what it means? Are you a runner?'

Jason smiled ruefully at her. 'I wish. I used to run a bit, but not these days. My back's a bit dodgy.' He shrugged. 'No idea what it means. Just kids playing some kind of stupid prank, I guess.'

Detective Riggs frowned at him again and then snapped her notebook shut. 'That's all I need for now, thank you. I'll be in touch.'

———

Back at the office, Jason checked his phone. *Shit.* Ten missed calls. That was about normal most days. He checked through the list and made a few mental notes to call people back. But there were more important things to think about right now. He checked his emails and texts. As usual, there was a jumble of unread correspondence. He'd wade through them all later. Except for the ones from his kids, he'd read them right away.

There was a text from Inga. He smiled. His daughter was always more important than whatever else was going on. Even if that was vandalism on the building site. He clicked open the message. *I've got to work this afternoon. Sally will give me a lift.* He sighed with relief. As much as he wanted to hang out with Inny, it was going to be a long day. She'd also sent him some kind of little video. He couldn't work out how to open it. Damn. He'd have to get Rachel to open it later on. He tapped out a quick message. *Love you Inny, see you tomorrow.* He thought about texting Jaxson as well, but then he checked his watch. Jax would be in a tennis coaching session right now. He smiled with pride at the thought of his talented son. He'd text him later on.

For now, he had to focus on work, so he pulled his mind off his kids and back to the list of things he'd planned to get done that morning. He couldn't concentrate. The mess at the building site kept flashing through his mind. He was annoyed about the delay, but more than that, he was curious about who was behind the destruction. The detective was right. It was his building site, so more than likely it was someone he'd pissed off. But he couldn't think who that might be. For better or worse, he tended to think the best of people, even though it meant his expectations were often unmet. But even though he racked his brain, he couldn't think of anyone that might have that kind of grudge against him.

The other likely explanation was someone wanted to delay his building project and get theirs finished first. This time he could think of a few people who weren't that thrilled about it. There was Brian, of course. Brian wasn't an idiot; he would want to finish his project first, get the best tenants and sell the apartments at the best prices. But Brian was notorious for trying to cut costs by underpaying tradies or trying to get cheap materials, which meant delays when tradies didn't want to work for him anymore, or when the cheap materials turned out to be defective and had to be replaced. Jason was pretty confident Brian didn't have a hope of finishing his project before his but even so, he was pretty sure Brian wasn't behind the vandalism. He was stubborn, but he wasn't mean. Besides, whoever had vandalised the site had really put a lot of effort in to messing things up. That wasn't Brian's style – he was too lazy. Plus, they still got on pretty well, even though they were rivals. Just last week they'd seen each other at a party and had had a great chat. Well, they'd given each other a fair bit of shit, but it was all good-natured. He'd thought so at the time, anyway.

There was plenty of other development going on at Golden Sands, though. Maybe one of the other developers saw him as a rival and wanted to send a warning? Jason thought about the other developers he knew. There was a local businessman who was building a shopping centre nearby. He'd been mad at Jason because he'd bought the block of land that he wanted, but that was over a year ago now. He'd ended up building the shopping centre on a different site, which turned out to be even better, so there were no hard feelings there. Jason certainly couldn't picture any of the other developers sneaking around his build site with a sledgehammer and a can of red paint. Most of them were older guys who almost never left their comfortable offices, anyway.

Then there was the strange message. *Run run run, you can't outrun me.* What the hell did that mean? Jason shrugged. He turned the words over and over in his mind, but they didn't suggest anything to him. It was just a stupid prank, he reminded himself. It didn't imply anything. Just someone trying to get under his skin. And anyway, the police were onto things now. They'd find whoever was behind the damage. That Detective Riggs looked like she was good at her job.

The rest of the day passed in a blur. Jason fielded phone calls, rescheduled tradies, spoke to detectives and made countless arrangements. Through it all, his mind turned over the events of the morning, but nothing seemed any clearer. Around lunchtime, Frank phoned. Jason picked up on the second ring.

'Hey boss. Just wanted to let you know the cops have questioned everyone on site, and no-one saw anything. We're back into the work, but they've still got that area of the site roped off with that police tape stuff. We'll fix it up when they let us back in there.'

They chatted for a few minutes about work details. 'Thanks Frank. Double-check the security fence tonight when you lock up, can you?' Jason asked before he rang off.

———

Later that afternoon, Jason pulled out of the parking lot, a knot of tension in his chest. For a moment, the old, familiar longing welled up in him. His old favourite watering hole, Chester's Beach Bar, was just three blocks away. He could pop in for a quick drink. It had been a long day. Just for a beer or two, enough to wash away the tight feeling in his chest. He sighed, turning his car in the opposite direction. There were enough long, beer-and-whiskey-soaked nights in his past. He couldn't open that door again. It was okay every now and again on a night out with his mates, but he wasn't going to start drinking alone. Not again. He had his kids to think about these days. Inga and Jaxson. Jax and Inny. Just the thought of them made him smile. He turned the car onto the main street and headed north.

His phone rang, routed through the in car system that Jaxson had helped him set up. Jason hit the button on his steering wheel and answered the call.

'Hello Jason, Detective Riggs here.' The voice filled the car speakers.

'Detective, what can I do for you? You caught the bad guys already?' Jason laughed.

Detective Riggs apparently did lack a sense of humour. 'No. I'm just calling with an update. We've had forensics on the site. Whoever did the damage didn't leave anything behind. There are some security cameras outside at the bank just down the street. Those cameras catch a large part of your front fence. We've pulled the footage, but there's nothing there either.'

'Okay. No fingerprints? Isn't that what you guys do?'

'There are many, many fingerprints in the area,' Riggs continued in her deadpan voice. 'If the vandal, or vandals, for that matter, had left behind a tool, say a paintbrush or hammer, then we might have been able to get prints. But due to the number of people that have access to the site, there's no use in getting prints from the various surfaces.'

'Right. So you're telling me it's going to be hard to track down whoever did this?' Jason asked.

'Yes. We're still running down a couple of leads, but we don't have much to go on at this stage.' Riggs paused for a moment. 'I think the biggest clue at this stage is the message on the wall. The vandal left it there for a reason. Have you thought what it could mean? Maybe something related to your past?'

Jason frowned. 'Nope, still no idea what that means.' He'd been thinking about it all day and was no closer to understanding why the vandal might have written the cryptic message. *Run run run.* It was so vague. He didn't run these days, and he certainly wasn't trying to outrun anyone. Not even metaphorically. But then again, maybe it was something from a long time ago. His childhood? A flash of memory darted across his mind. But why would an incident from way back then have anything to do with the damage at the construction site? Of course it didn't. It was just a stupid coincidence.

'Well, if you think of anything, give me a call,' Detective Riggs said. And she rang off, leaving the beeping of the phone echoing through the car.

CHAPTER 3

He used to run everywhere. That was one of his strongest childhood memories. Jason didn't spend much time thinking about the past; he wasn't one for reminiscing. He liked to live in the present and think about the future. But when he did think back, that was the way he remembered himself as a child. Running. He had no patience for walking. Life was full of adventures, and you weren't going to fit them all in unless you were fast.

He knew this from a young age. And so he ran. Down the cracked footpaths of Woodridge, past the rows of weatherboard houses with peeling paint, he ran. Even in the summer heat that felt as though it would strip the skin from your bones, he ran. He could feel the warmth of the concrete footpath through the soles of his trainers. He ran in the house, despite his mother scolding him and telling him not to thunder about like an elephant. But there was always something he wanted to do. He'd slide on the lino floor in his socks, into his younger brother's room. He'd run down to the neighbours, darting under the sprinkler to cool down. He'd slow to a walk long enough to say hello to the neighbour, Mr Smith, who would stand on the steps watering his lawn with a long green hose, cracked in a few places and squirting waterfalls onto the path. Mr Smith would wipe the sweat from his forehead, and say, 'It's hot enough to fry an egg on the footpath, isn't it, Jason?' Then Jason's eyes would go wide with wonder as he thought about getting an egg from the high shelf where his mother kept them and trying it out. He might just do that later on. Then he would nod to Mr Smith and launch back into a run.

Blinking away the memories, Jason gazed up at the sky, which was streaked with the oranges and pinks of sunset. He was sitting on the back deck of his beachside home. His house was quiet and peaceful. Just the way he'd left it. It was his oasis of calm. As well as being beautiful inside, it also had a great view of the beach. There was still enough light to see clearly, and the beach was full of people walking, making sandcastles, even swimming. He loved the long summer days on the Sunshine Coast, and this was his favourite time of day. When the light was golden and soft and the people on the beach were tired and happy. Or maybe his favourite time of day was early morning, when the waves were pounding and he could grab his board for a quick surf before work. He smiled to himself. Really, any time of day was pretty spectacular here. Not too bad for a boy from a housing commission unit in Woodridge.

He shook off the memories of his childhood and thought about the day. The dripping red letters on the build site seemed like they might be a threat, but he couldn't imagine who would want to threaten him. Still, the reference to running had stirred up all kinds of childhood memories. A random vandal with some kind of grudge against him wouldn't know about him running a lot as a kid, though. It was a coincidence. The memories hung around like smoke drifting in the wind. Maybe it was just a sign that he hadn't seen his family for a while. He should go and see his parents on the weekend. And Nan Dooksie. He always loved visiting her. Just thinking of his gentle Nan brought a smile to his face.

He took a quick glance at his phone. Inga would still be at work and Jaxson would be doing homework. He'd check in with them both a bit later on. For the moment, he felt like he needed to think through the events of the day. Later, he had to get himself some dinner and make a few phone calls. But for now, there was just enough time to go for a walk on the beach. He'd sit out on the sand and watch as the inky-blue twilight spread across the sky. He'd watch the tourists drift off to the hotels and restaurants and wait until he could see the first stars appear in the sky. Then he'd come back home and get out the guitar. The perfect end to a rough day. That was just what he needed to clear his head.

———

Down by the water, the sand rough underneath his bare feet, Jason let his mind wander. More memories of childhood skittered through his thoughts. He remembered his childhood house, compared it to the beautiful townhouse he lived in now. The house in Woodridge , where he'd grown up, felt like a world away. It had been a scrappy, seventies brick-and-tile, a housing commission house in the middle of a sea of similar houses. He could still remember the half-dead lawn and the front path scattered with the bikes he and his brothers had dropped. The red geraniums in the garden by the front porch were rangy and in need of watering. But that front porch was always swept to within an inch of its life.

In those halcyon days, he and his brothers were always together. They were always wrestling, always scheming, always running from one adventure to another. One of the kids down the street, a perpetually sunburnt boy called Richie, had a pool, making him a god among the neighbourhood children. Jason was silver-tongued, even then, and he could always talk his way into being invited to swim in the tepid water, his brothers trailing behind him.

Sometimes Richie would be generous and let Pauly and a few other kids from the neighbourhood in - and sometimes not. But they always made the most of it when they did get a chance. They would swim until their fingers wrinkled and their eyes stung from the chlorine. They did bombies and threw each other in, laughed and splashed until the pull of hunger drove them home to find some dinner. Even in the late afternoon, the scorching Queensland sun would have them almost dry by the time they'd walked the half a block to the squat housing commission bungalow. By then, their mum would be in her usual spot in the kitchen, completely unbothered by the fact she didn't know where her kids had been. They were somewhere in the neighbourhood, and they were pretty good at looking after each other. Even if they did squabble and wrestle constantly.

The backyard had been tiny, just enough for a swing set and a trampoline. Jason smiled to himself. They'd had some fun times in that house. He thought of the banana swing on the old swing set, Matt and Ryan holding down the corner poles as he got it going as high as he could, determined to get the swing to go up and over the top of the railing, a full 360-degree curve. He'd given it a huge burst of energy and the swing went up in a big arc and then stopped, something in the mechanism preventing it from going over the top. He'd been catapulted through the air, lucky to have a soft landing on the grass and not break both of his legs on the concrete of the back patio. It had winded him, but before long he was back on the swing set, determined to get it up and over the top this time.

The house always felt too small to contain the energy of three boys. Their mother was constantly in the kitchen, usually stirring at something on the stove. She'd put up with their roughhousing and wrestling as they watched cartoons, sprawled on the shag pile carpet of the lounge room. But then she'd tell them to go outside, send them to their rooms, or threaten to swat them with the wooden spoon she wielded like a baton. It was bluster, Jason knew, just a ploy to keep them in line and stop them from breaking the furniture. But there was always a moment when a note of irritation would creep into her voice. Or maybe it was a slight change in her pitch. Then it was time to take her seriously or suffer the consequences.

Sometimes, in the middle of a fierce wrestle with one of his brothers, Jason would ignore the sixth sense that told him his mother meant business. Then, before they had the chance to run, she'd be out from behind the kitchen bench, dispensing justice. She was tough, his mother. He always knew that. Jason felt a little rush of gratitude for her. She could be blunt, and sometimes he disagreed with her, but she'd always been a solid presence in his life. He remembered the days before Ivan had come into their lives, when it had been just him and his brothers and his mum. She'd handled everything, keeping them fed and happy and – most of the time – well behaved. They'd never felt as though they were missing out on anything. Now, in retrospect, he could see just how hard she had worked and how much she'd given them.

Jason was grateful for Ivan, too. He'd been a caring and constant presence in their lives ever since he and Jason's mum got married. And the two new younger siblings who came later were a welcome addition to the family. Now, as an adult, he felt like he'd won the jackpot when it came to his family.

The neighbourhood kids sometimes asked where his dad was. He'd just shrug. He didn't know most of the time, and he didn't care all of the time. The man was a vague presence in their lives, someone who turned up from time to time, expecting them to welcome him back with open arms. Jason searched his childhood memories for some feeling of anger or resentment or sorrow about his father; the man he now thought of as just a sperm donor. There was nothing there. The only emotion he remembered feeling toward him was irritation. Irritation that he came back into their lives when they were doing just fine without him. Jason remembered feeling annoyed that he seemed to expect accolades for doing any small thing for them, and he'd spark with anger whenever they didn't respond with joy at his very presence. His mother didn't rant or rave at her absent husband, but Jason could see the tension in her shoulders and in the way she held the knife as she diced carrots and potatoes for their dinner. She deserved better. Even as a kid he knew that.

One day, his father came bounding through the front door after being absent for weeks, maybe even months. He told the three boys who were eating their Weet-Bix at the melamine table in the kitchen that he had a surprise for them. 'I'm going to take you horse riding.'

They looked at him sceptically, doubtful this would be the adventure he promised. Jason could remember the frown that crossed the man's face when he understood they weren't excited at the idea. He pressed on regardless, telling the boys to get ready. They did as they were told, curious enough about a new activity to give it a try even though it promised to be far more sedate than the motorbikes or go-karts they'd hoped for. Jason remembered the rest of the day clearly – the fat ponies they rode were slow and lazy, and the instructor kept telling them not to shout or be too boisterous. Worse still, Jason's eyes and nose started to itch and before long he could barely see through his puffy eyes. By the end of the horse ride, the boys were all complaining and their father was angry. After that, they didn't see him again for months.

They didn't need him, though. Jason knew that from a young age. They had each other, and they had their mother. It was enough. She must have found it hard, with three reckless boys fighting their way through the house and through their lives. Not that she showed it. But now, as he thought back, he realised how much she'd shouldered to keep them fed, clean and in line. But there were moments that stood out in Jason's memory, like their Friday fish and chips nights. Their mother would pile them into the station wagon and they'd slide on the vinyl seats, ramming each other into the doors each time the car went around a corner. Then, at Woodridge Fish and Chips, they would pile through the doors, begging their mother for coins to feed the pinball machine while they waited for their order number to be called. Jason could still remember the crisp, salty chips and the battered fish that tasted, in his memory, better than anything he'd ever eaten. They'd eat from the greaseproof paper and newspaper that the fish and chips came wrapped in, squabbling over the chips like seagulls. Their mother would smile at them and scold them affectionately, laughing along with their jokes. It was in those moments that Jason had been sure, even as a boy, that they had everything they needed. Just the four of them, in the middle of Woodridge, was all he wanted. He'd been happy.

———

Jason shook his head, clearing away the childhood memories. It wasn't often he let himself think about his past. No good wallowing in what had been. He tried to keep looking forward, thinking about the next project, the next thing he wanted to work on. He always had a hundred new ideas fighting for purchase in his mind, each one trying to outweigh the others. There was no time to be thinking about back then. But for some reason, the strange message on the wall of the build site had stirred up his memory. Who the hell could have vandalised the site? Was it really someone who had it in for him? Jason shook his head. Of course not. That was ridiculous. It was probably just neighbourhood kids, out to stir trouble or channel some kind of horror movie. There were plenty of kids like that in Golden Sands, at a loose end on a Friday night.

His thoughts wandered back to the night before. Dinner with the guys, then wandering the streets with Pauly as though they were teenagers again. The day had been so busy he hadn't had much time to think about the skinny man at the Galaxy, and the frightened girl. What was her name? Stella, that was it. There was definitely something off about that place. He thought about how the club had been half empty, and how the bar tenders were standing around chatting rather than working. And Friday night should have been their busiest night, too. He shrugged. Hopefully it wouldn't be long until the old club closed down. It would be a problem having such an eyesore just down the road from his development, not to mention the potential noise issues. Probably not a bad thing if it shut, someone could buy it and do something else with the site. He stopped, the idea hitting him like a punch. Of course. *He* should buy it.

It was a perfect idea. He ran through all of the things he could do with a prime site like that. Another apartment block. A shopping complex. Housing, parking, garage, office space. There were so many possibilities. The wheels in his mind had started whirling, and his childhood was instantly forgotten. The future beckoned. There was no use living in the past. He continued walking along the stretch of beach for a few more minutes, thinking of what else he could do with the old nightclub. Then, resolved, he turned back toward home. Tomorrow, he'd find a real estate agent and see if he could set the wheels in motion.

CHAPTER 4

'Hey boss, you'd better come and take a look at this,' Frank's voice echoed down the phone line. It was early in the morning, far earlier than the foreman usually called. 'There's, well… look, I think you should come see for yourself.'

'Right. I'll be there in ten,' Jason replied. The note of urgency in Frank's voice made him instantly curious – Frank was usually competent and could manage most of the little issues that came up on site. Maybe this was a bigger issue that needed Jason's input. It had been over a week since the graffiti incident, and even though the police hadn't caught the vandals, they'd moved on. The project was back on schedule, as surprising as that was for a big job like this.

Jason had already been driving toward the office when the phone rang, so he changed lanes and turned back toward the building site. There was a bit of traffic on the road, but at this time of morning, it wasn't too bad. Golden Sands was vibrant and full of life, but it was also a tourist town. Lots of people slept in and started their days late. One day, Jason thought, he'd do the same. For now, he liked to get a jump on the traffic, and that meant leaving early.

Jason pulled to a stop at the front of the site and got out of the car. He was looking forward to seeing the progress on the project. They'd repaired the damage that had been done when the site was vandalised. It had taken a few days of everyone working overtime to catch up, but lucky for him, his team was willing to go the extra mile. Jason had driven past Brian Welsh's development recently, and even from what he could see from the car, it was clear that Brian was behind schedule. The thought of it brought a smile to his face. Jason was sure he'd beat Brian to the finish line. Happy buyers would be moving into his apartments before Brian even got his on the market, he was sure.

Jason nodded to some of the workers milling around the site. He said hi to a few of the guys he knew by name, but with a job like this, there were plenty he didn't know. Even this early, there were half a dozen tradies all hanging around the main entrance. Something felt off. They were all just standing around, not actually doing any work. Were they waiting for something? Maybe they were waiting for Frank to give them their orders. Wasting time like this pissed him off. He'd see what was bothering Frank, and then get them back on the job.

Jason had every sympathy for the workers, who were the backbone of his project. He'd been a chippie himself at the start of his career, and knew how demanding the work could be. He always made sure his crew were treated well and paid well, but he expected them to work hard, too, not just stand around gossiping. 'Over here, boss,' Frank called.

Jason followed the sound of Frank's voice, noticing a hum of tension in the air. Something was going on, that was for sure. He came around a corner and felt as though he'd been punched in the ribs. *Fuck, not again.* Smashed pipes, broken framework, broken glass and splashes of red paint were everywhere. Jason let out a low whistle. This was worse than the first time. Someone had really done a number on this place. Frank was standing in the middle of the mess, a serious look on his face. He had his arms crossed across his chest. Jason turned to see the wall behind him. Once again, there was a message scrawled across the wall in dripping red paint. This time, it read *Pride goes before a fall. Watch out you don't fall and break your head.* The dark red of the paint looked eerily like blood.

What the fuck...' Jason muttered. He turned to Frank. 'Was it like this when you got here?'

'Yeah, boss. Timmons was first on site this morning, I was off getting materials. He called me right away.'

Timmons was one of the long-term chippies on Jason's crew. He had a set of keys for the security gates.

'The glass is from some windows that were getting put in today.'

Jason frowned. Windows weren't cheap. Fixing all this damage wouldn't be cheap, either. Plus, it meant playing catch-up again. 'Who's been in here?'

'A few of the fellas. Timmons, too, of course. I didn't call the police yet, wanted to show you first.'

There was a note of caution in Frank's voice. Jason wondered if Frank expected him to hide this mess from the police. Why would he do that? Only if he was involved in something dodgy – which he wasn't. Of course he was going to call the cops.

'Right. I'll phone them, then I'll talk to Timmons. Where is he?'

Frank nodded. 'Out the back having a smoke, boss. Reckon it rattled him a bit, finding the place like this. Now you're here, I'll get everyone back to work.'

'Good. Just keep them out of this area, of course.' Jason called over one of the apprentices who was gawking at the mess from the doorway. 'Jonesy, I'm going out the back. Can you stay in this area? Make sure no-one touches anything until the police get here.' He was a good kid, not much older than Jason's son.

Jonesy nodded earnestly. 'Sure, Jason.' He took up his post, standing with his arms folded over his chest like a security guard. Jason smiled at the boy's serious expression and went to find Timmons. On the way, he found the phone number Detective Riggs had given him. He dialled as he walked through the building site. Riggs picked up on the second ring.

'Detective Riggs? We spoke about a week ago when my building site was vandalised.'

'Yes, I remember. What can I help you with, Jason?' She didn't waste time with pleasantries.

'We've had another incident. Same kind of vandalism.'

'Hmm. We'll be right there. Have you phoned it through on the regular police line?'

'No, I thought I should report it straight to you.'

She made a small noise that could have been agreement or annoyance, Jason wasn't sure. Then she said, 'Make sure no-one touches anything. We'll be there soon.'

Jason walked out of what would be the back entrance to the apartment complex into the yard, which would one day feature a pool and garage for the residents. For now, it was a dusty patch of dirt ringed with high security fences and filled with building supplies.

Timmons was one of the older men on the crew, probably in his fifties. Jason found him at the back of the yard, sitting on a pallet of bricks.

'Hey boss.' He waved his cigarette. 'Sorry, I don't normally smoke. It just shook me up a bit, ya know? Finding the site damaged like that. Who would do something like that? Those letters… I thought it was blood at first.' He shivered, then took another drag on his cigarette.

Jason shrugged. 'I don't know, mate, but when I find them…' His tone was filled with resolve. He wasn't the kind of guy who got angry quickly. In fact, he could usually see the humour in a situation, but he wasn't laughing now. Someone had fucked with his build site twice now, and he was going to get to the bottom of it. 'Frank said you were the first on site this morning?'

Timmons nodded. 'Yeah. There were a couple of blokes waiting out the front, but I unlocked the security fence and they went straight out the back. I was the first one to go inside. Went in to check the fellas had finished off the plumbing in that room, and that's when I found the mess. Got a hell of a shock.'

'The fence was locked as normal when you got here? No signs anyone had broken in?'

Timmons shrugged. 'Nah. Everything seemed just like normal, Jason. I mean, except for that room. All that paint on the wall, too. Do you think someone's trying to send us a message?'

Jason frowned. 'No. I think someone's trying to send *me* a message.'

———

Detective Riggs looked over the scene with her customary frown. She had two other police detectives with her this time. One was the tall offsider who'd been there last time, and the other was a younger, blond man with a camera. They were both inspecting the broken glass and pipes, taking photos and making notes. It was a warm, balmy day but here, inside the concrete structure of the building, it was cool. Jason felt a shiver run up his spine. He walked over to where the two detectives were standing, feeling the crunch of broken glass underfoot. As soon as the cops were gone, he'd get in here with a broom himself. Last thing he needed was someone getting injured on the glass.

'Looks like you might need to upgrade your security. Get some cameras,' Riggs said to him in her dry tone.

'Yeah, I'm onto it,' Jason said. He'd phoned Rachel on his way back into the site and asked her to look into it. Anything tech related was not his strong point. And that was understating it a bit. He knew his weaknesses, and he'd leave that with Rachel. She'd been sympathetic about the vandalism, and she'd known exactly who to call. 'Leave it with me, Jason. I'll get a technician around to install a set of cameras today.'

Jason had told Frank to keep an eye out for the security techs, and to work with them to get the cameras in place. He turned his attention back to Riggs. 'Any idea who might be behind this?'

Detective Riggs frowned. 'No. Still no leads since last time we were here. We'll gather as much evidence as we can, of course, but I don't think we're going to find out much.' She waved her pen at the room. 'It looks like the vandal didn't leave anything behind. We'll keep looking of course, but I don't see the paint can or paintbrush. Just like last time. And my guess would be that even if we did find something left behind, they probably wore gloves. We'll pull the security footage from the buildings along the street, but once again, I don't think it will tell us much.' She paused to make a note with her pencil in the little notebook. 'Your foreman says the site was locked up securely when the first workers arrived?' She said it like a question.

'Yeah. I've done a walk around the perimeter fence, too. No sign that anyone's forced their way in.'

Riggs cocked an eyebrow at him. 'The fence wouldn't be impossible to climb, but it would take someone pretty agile.' She frowned at him. 'You have a big crew here, don't you? Any of them have an issue with you?'

Jason shook his head firmly. 'No. I treat my crew fairly, and they're all good guys.'

She nodded slowly. 'Well, who has keys for the security fence?'

'Frank. Timmons. About three other guys. Frank can get you a list of names but they've all been working with me for years. I trust them.'

The detective nodded, making a note in her book. 'I'll get the names from your foreman.' She paused for a moment, looking over at the red words scrawled across the wall. 'Strange message. Does it mean anything to you?'

Jason looked at the words. He shook his head. 'No clue. Just someone trying to be smart, I guess.' He ran a hand over his head, feeling a prickle of irritation.

'Break your head. Normally, the saying is break your neck. I wonder why it's phrased like that?'

Jason shrugged. 'No idea. Like I said, probably just kids trying to be smart-arses.'

Riggs nodded. 'Okay.' She turned away and looked at the message again, cocking her head to one side. Then she turned back to him. 'I think we're nearly done here. If you think of anything else, let me know.'

Jason let his gaze sweep over the room. The broken glass, the shattered pipes, the dripping red of the paint on the wall – beneath it all, he could feel an itching sensation, like there was something he should be thinking of. *Break your head.* Riggs was right. There was something off about the phrasing. But it was probably just kids playing stupid mind games. He turned his back on the vandalised room and headed back through the building site. He was going to find out who'd done this. And make them pay.

———

Back at the office, Jason stopped at Rachel's desk for a quick chat. She filled him in on some details of other projects he had going on. There was nothing that needed his attention at the moment. Jason was not interested in micromanaging his businesses. He hired good people and was happy to give them the space they needed to get their work done. In fact, he often thought his true talents lay in finding the right person to do a job and bringing out the best in them. Much better than him trying to do the job himself and getting in the way.

Jason checked his calendar. He'd planned to be on the building site today, so there wasn't anything major scheduled. He sat down at the desk and scrolled through his unread messages. He clicked open one from Inga. *Hey Dad. Have you watched that TikTok I sent you?* He had no idea what a TikTok was, and he had no desire to find out.

Not yet. Dinner tonight? Then you can show me in person. I'll see if Jax is free too, he texted back. It didn't take long for her reply to come through. *Sounds great. I'll get a lift from work and see you there.*

Jason texted the dinner plans through to Jaxson and then scrolled through the rest of his messages. There was a WhatsApp message from Pauly in the group chat he had going with some of his mates. *Heard you had some trouble at the building site. Everything okay?*

He frowned, wondering how the news could have reached Pauly. Then he shook his head. It had to be someone on his crew. He'd worked with some of the same guys for years and considered them mates. But on a building site, gossip and secrets were traded like currency. There were plenty of the crew that knew Pauly too. One of them must have told him. Not that he cared that much, but sometimes it irritated him a bit.

Jason thought over the events of the morning. Detective Riggs didn't seem very enthusiastic about finding who was behind the damage at the site, and she didn't seem to think they had much to go on. But Jason wasn't content with that. He was determined to get to the bottom of the situation. There was something nagging in the back of his mind about the message that had been painted on the wall. It might help to talk it over with someone, he thought. And Pauly was always good for a chat. He tapped out a quick text. *Yeah, a bit of trouble, but nothing major. Free for lunch? I'll tell you all about it then.*

The reply came through straight away. *Yep. The usual place?* Jason smiled, and texted back. *Perfect. See you there.*

———

The usual place was a pub near the beach. A big, airy building full of tourists with sandy feet and locals who liked the ambience. It served great, old-school fish and chips with crispy batter, and perfect Aussie hamburgers stacked high with salad, bacon, melted cheese and, of course, beetroot. He and his mates often met there for lunch on the weekends. The Wolf Pack. He smiled at the thought.

His group of old high school mates called themselves the Wolf Pack. It was just a stupid name, really, a tongue-in-cheek joke one of them had made years ago that had stuck. But still, he knew there was no-one he'd trust more to have his back than the guys in the Wolf Pack. They'd been mates for years, and beyond the bickering and the teasing, the stupid fights over trivial things and the times when they'd go for weeks without talking as their lives filled with work, families, kids and commitments – beyond all that there was a foundation of trust that had been built over years of knowing each other. Sometimes they gave him the shits, but most of the time, Jason was grateful to have them in his life.

Pauly was waiting for him at an outside table, his legs stretched out in the sunshine. Back in high school, Pauly had been lean and tanned from long days spent surfing and playing footy in the sun. These days, he wasn't quite as lean and his tan could use some work. But he still had the same ready smile and quick, cheeky wit. ''Bout time you got here,' he said when he saw Jason. 'I'm starving and need a beer. You're buying, right?' He laughed.

They ordered their food and the waiter brought their drinks over straight away. A pint of mid strength for Pauly and water for Jason. His younger self would have laughed at the thought of drinking water when you could drink beer, but these days he tried to be moderate, especially on work days. Their burgers weren't far behind. Pauly drank nearly half of his beer in one go, then settled back in his chair. They chatted for a few minutes as they ate, about the kids and the surf. When the kids had been younger, they'd swap stories of the horrors of sleepless nights, toilet training and general toddler mayhem. Pauly's kids were roughly the same age as Inny and Jax. These days, they were both proud of their confident, accomplished kids. Jason secretly thought his kids were the best, but he'd admit he might be a tiny bit biased.

'So, what's been going on with your project?' Pauly asked. 'I heard you had a few issues?'

Jason rolled his eyes. 'Who told you that? One of the crew from the site?'

Pauly laughed. 'Yeah, Frank's wife is friends with Shaz. She phoned Shaz and told her all about it, and Shaz told me.'

Sharon, better known as Shaz, was Pauly's wife. She was a rosy-cheeked brunette who looked sweet and innocent, but was as tough as anyone Jason knew. She could hold her own with any of the boys when it came to drinking, giving each other shit, or even arm wrestling.

Jason told Pauly all about the vandalism on the site and the strange messages on the wall. 'First one was *Run, run, run, you can't outrun me.* I mean, you know how much I used to run around when I was a kid. I kind of thought it might be something to do with that.'

Pauly laughed. 'Man, you were always running. My mum used to call you the roadrunner.'

Jason laughed, too. 'Yeah, well, I'm not so sure now. The second message was just some stupid shit. It was *Pride goes before a fall. Watch out you don't fall and break your head.* Just a dumb warning that could apply to anyone.'

Pauly chewed thoughtfully on a crispy, golden chip. 'Remember that time you fell out of a second storey window? You were sitting in the window and you leant back against the flyscreen or something like that.'

The memory came back to Jason in a flash. He could still remember the feeling of utter shock he felt when the flyscreen gave way and he seemed to hang for a moment in thin air, arms flailing like a cartoon character, before he plummeted down to the ground below. He'd narrowly missed landing on the concrete edge of the garden bed.

'Didn't you land on your head?' Pauly asked.

'Yeah, I did. Knocked myself clean out, and ended up spending two days in hospital,' Jason laughed. He'd actually enjoyed the time in hospital, eating cups of fruit and jelly and trying his best to flirt with the pretty nurses, even though he'd been just a kid.

'I wonder if the message has anything to do with that?' Pauly mused.

Jason shook his head. 'Maybe. I doubt it. How many people in my life would remember that stupid incident? Probably only a handful. I didn't even remember it myself.'

'Yeah, true. And how likely is it that someone who knows about it has a grudge against you now?'

Jason shrugged and laughed, and the conversation moved on to something else. But for the rest of the afternoon, the words swirled around in his mind. *Watch out you don't fall and break your head.* What did it mean? And who was behind the cryptic messages? He didn't have the faintest clue, but he was sure as hell going to find out.

CHAPTER 5

Jason spent the afternoon walking around Golden Sands, in the area near his development. It was time to ask some questions. Maybe someone nearby had seen something that would help him find out who had been vandalising his site. The first place he went into was a gourmet deli just across the road. It was an upmarket place, the kind that sold fresh native flowers and organic goats' cheese. Usually, that kind of place was too pretentious for Jason, but he enjoyed having a little poke around the shelves. The next time he was trying to impress a girlfriend with breakfast, he'd pop in here for some maple-cured prosciutto and a loaf of their house-made sourdough. Behind the counter, the young woman who greeted him had a colourful scarf twisted through her pink and green hair and rings in each perfectly arched eyebrow.

'Hi, can I help you find something?' she asked, in a bright voice.

'Yeah, I'm just looking for some information,' Jason said. He explained who he was and pointed toward the building site, visible through the shop windows if you looked past the fresh flowers and baskets full of baguettes. Jason gave a brief explanation of the vandalism that had been taking place on the site, and the girl's eyes grew wide.

'Oh shit, that doesn't sound very good,' she said.

'Well, I'm just wondering if you or any of the other staff might have seen anything?'

She shook her head. 'Nah. Not if it happened at night time. I don't live around here. I could ask the boss, though. She lives in an apartment above the shop and knows most things that go on around here. Hang on, and I'll get her.'

The girl hurried through a door behind the counter and after a few moments came back with an older woman following her. The woman was wearing a blue silk blouse and tailored black pants, and had a slight expression of annoyance on her face. Jason smiled at her, taking it as a challenge to get her on side.

'It's a beautiful shop you have here,' he started. 'Really great selection of stuff.' The woman's face thawed a bit, and she smiled at him. They chatted for a few moments about the challenges of getting a really good loaf of bread, and how quickly the neighbourhood was changing. More people cared about that kind of stuff these days. She was smiling openly at him by now, but as Jason began to explain about the building site and the vandalism, the smile slipped away.

'Oh no,' she said, 'I haven't noticed anything out of place. This is a very good neighbourhood, you know. Very quiet. We don't have any issues around here.'

'No worries, just thought I'd ask,' Jason said. 'Thanks anyway.' He turned to walk toward the door, and as he did, he caught sight of the Galaxy Nightclub through the window. He turned back around. 'Just one more question. Do you know anything about the old nightclub? Know who owns it?'

For a brief second, an expression of alarm crossed the woman's face, and then she folded her arms across her chest. 'No. I don't know anything about the Galaxy at all.' Then she turned away from him and stalked out of the room.

———

Jason asked at a few other shops and cafes in the area, but no-one had seen anything that could shed any light on the vandalism at the building site. At first, he thought he must have imagined the look of alarm on the face of the woman in the deli, but a man behind the counter of a clothing store looked distinctly nervous when he asked about the Galaxy. And a woman in a cafe refused to answer his question and asked him to leave. Something was definitely off.

After a few more stops, Jason went to a juice bar to cool off. He bought a tropical mix and sat outside in the courtyard to drink it. As if on cue, his phone rang. Rachel.

'Ro Ro. How are ya?' He had a habit of giving nicknames to the people he cared about, and Rachel was no exception. She was always dignified and elegant, but she took his nicknames in her stride.

'Hello Jason. I was just phoning to let you know that the new security cameras have been installed, and they're working well. They've got motion sensors attached to them, and if they're triggered, the video feed will go straight to a computer here in the office.'

'Rachel, you're the best. What would I do without you?' He was always so grateful for her. He'd have to give her a raise. Or had he already done that recently? Anyway, it didn't matter. She deserved another raise.

'I'm sure you'd be fine without me, Jason. But that's not a problem, easily done. How is your afternoon going?'

'Kinda weird, actually.' He told Rachel about talking to the shopkeepers close to the building site, and about how some of them had reacted when he asked about the Galaxy. 'It was as if they were nervous about talking about the place. That's weird, right?'

Rachel was slow to jump to conclusions, as always. 'Perhaps. But maybe you just got them when they were busy, or maybe they don't like the place because it's an eyesore.'

Jason remembered what he'd been thinking about the night before. 'You know what I was just thinking, I should buy the place. Would be great, wouldn't it? I could redevelop, turn it into a nice restaurant or something. Oh, I know! A microbrewery. They're hot right now.'

Rachel laughed. 'One project at a time, Jason.'

He smiled. 'Yeah, yeah, the octopus of opportunity and all that. I know, I know. Still, now that I think of it, real estate agents know most things that go on in a neighbourhood. Maybe I should talk to one and see if they know anything.'

'That's true. Good idea actually.' It was high praise, coming from her.

'See, I'm full of good ideas. So, how do I find the best real estate agent in the area?'

'Hold on a minute,' Rachel said. On the other end of the line, Jason could hear her keyboard clattering as she typed. After a few moments, she said, 'I've just texted the number to your phone. By the look of things, this woman was the best-selling real estate agent in Golden Sands last year.'

'Rach, have I told you you're the best?'

'Once or twice, Jason, once or twice.' And then she rang off.

———

Jason opened the message and found a contact for someone called Mia Sellars, Golden Sands Real Estate. No time like the present. He dialled the number and asked the perky-sounding receptionist if Mia would have a few minutes to talk with him.

'Of course. Come past the office, she's in right now and I'm sure she'll be able to fit you in for a quick chat.'

That was good news. Jason liked it when things moved quickly. Within minutes he was standing in front of Golden Sands Real Estate. It was in one of the older parts of the suburb, well-established but quieter and less touristy. Jason walked in and was greeted by the receptionist he'd spoken to on the phone. She was young, probably in her early twenties, and was wearing a phone headset over her short-cropped hair. She smiled at Jason.

'Oh hey. Are you the guy I just spoke with on the phone? That was quick.'

'Yep, that's me,' he smiled.

'Well, Mia is in her office. I've told her you're on your way, so you can go right through if you like. Just through there.'

Jason went in the direction she'd pointed, into a big office with a huge window looking out toward the beach. There was expensive-looking art on the walls that really suited the decor, and a huge glass-topped desk. Jason was impressed by the office, but he was even more blown away by the woman sitting behind the desk. She stood to shake his hand, and he could see she was tall and slim. Her long, dark hair hung loose over her shoulders, and her eyes were striking and intense. The simple, sleeveless black dress she was wearing, with the skirt that finished at her knees, made her look even more classy. Jason resisted the urge to say *wow,* and instead shook Mia's hand. She had a firm handshake and fire-engine-red fingernails.

'Thanks for seeing me on such short notice. You must be Mia? I'm Jason.'

She smiled. 'Hi Jason. Why don't you take a seat? Are you looking to buy a house? Or maybe you're selling?'

'No, neither, actually,' he laughed. He told her about his development project.

'Right, I know the one. It's an impressive project. Looks like it's moving ahead pretty quickly, too.' She smiled warmly, and he felt like he'd do anything to make her smile again. He had to rein in his wandering mind and focus on the conversation.

'Well, it was. We've had a few problems with vandalism in the last week.' He gave her a quick run-down, aware that she probably had a busy day. She didn't seem rushed, though – in fact, she had an air of calmness about her. He liked that.

'That's unusual. We don't usually get much vandalism around this area. Although we are seeing a lot of new people and new businesses move into Golden Sands, so maybe things are changing a bit.' She frowned slightly at him.

'Well, that's one of the things I wanted to ask you about. You know the area pretty well, right? I've been asking around a few shops in the area, trying to find out if anyone saw anything out of the ordinary, and I haven't had much luck. Seems like everyone keeps to themselves and doesn't pay attention to what's going on outside their own little worlds.'

He thought for a moment of his childhood in Woodridge. You couldn't scratch your arse there without someone noticing and tattling on you. There were so many times in his childhood that he'd done something naughty – climbed onto the roof of the fish and chip shop, for example, or pissed in old Mrs Lombardi's rose bushes – and the news would travel so fast his mum would know about it before he even got home. She'd be standing by the front door as he came in, tapping one foot on the lino floor, and he'd know he was in trouble. But here… well, on some days, he thought you could commit a murder in broad daylight and no-one would even look up from their phones.

Mia laughed. 'Oh yes, that's totally what Golden Sands is like. Like that row of monkeys… what is it? See no evil, hear no evil, speak no evil. But if you want my advice, I'd ask around at nighttime. There are lot of businesses here, restaurants and bars, that only open in the evenings. You might find some of them a bit more observant when it comes to what's going on around them.'

Jason nodded. It was a good idea. She was smart as well as beautiful. 'Another question. Do you happen to know who owns the Galaxy Nightclub? It's just down from my build site.' He watched her closely, but she didn't seem to show any of the alarm that the other local businesspeople had shown at the mention of the Galaxy.

'The Galaxy?' She looked thoughtful. 'You know, that one is a bit of a mystery. Officially, it's owned by a shell company. Galaxy Holdings, I think it's called. Unofficially, the man who owns the place is known as Mr X. No-one really knows who he is, but apparently, he owns a bit of the real estate around here.' She gave Jason a mischievous smile. 'You know, I could probably find out for you, but it will cost you.'

Jason hoped she was flirting with him. 'Sure. Name your price. Anything at all.' He matched her mischievous smile with one of his own.

Then, all of a sudden, she was serious again. 'When it comes time to sell or rent the apartments and shops in your complex, you give me the exclusive listing.'

He laughed. Under the beautiful exterior she was a hard-nosed real estate agent through and through. He didn't mind. In fact, he'd been thinking he'd list the apartments with Golden Sands Real Estate before he even walked into Mia's office. Still, right now he was in a good position to negotiate. 'You drive a hard bargain, Mia. But you've got a deal, on one condition.'

She raised one eyebrow at him. 'Oh. And what condition is that?'

'You let me buy you a coffee some time.'

She pursed her lips in mock thoughtfulness, wrinkling her nose while she considered the proposition. Then she smiled. 'You drive a hard bargain yourself, Jason. But you've got a deal.' She stuck out her hand for him to shake., and glanced at her watch. 'And now, I'll have to excuse myself. I have a client coming through in five minutes, and I have some paperwork I need to get ready.'

'Absolutely.' Jason picked up a business card from the holder on her desk. 'Well, I've got your number now. I'll be in touch to organise that coffee. It was lovely to meet you, Mia.'

'It was nice to meet you too, Jason. And, for the record, I would have gone out for coffee with you anyway,' she winked.

Jason laughed. 'For the record, I was thinking of listing my apartments with you anyway. But now that I've met you in person, I'm absolutely planning on it. The coffee is a bonus.' He returned her wink, gave her a broad smile and walked out the room.

On the walk back to the car, Jason's phone rang. It was Detective Riggs. For a moment, he hoped she might have had a breakthrough in the investigation.

'Detective Riggs, how are you? Have you cracked the case, or are you ringing to tell me I've won the lotto?'

As usual, Riggs didn't display a sense of humour. 'The investigation is still continuing, Jason.' She paused for a moment. 'I've heard you've been out around the neighbourhood asking questions.'

'Well, news travels fast, detective. Just trying to get to know my new neighbours, you know.'

'You're interfering with our investigation, Jason. I'm the detective on this case, not you.' Her voice had a scolding tone to it, as though he were a naughty schoolboy. He'd been plenty naughty as boy, and hadn't paid much attention to scolding teachers back then. He certainly wasn't going to stammer and apologise now.

Jason laughed. 'Well, I'm not arguing with you there, Riggs. And there's no law against me chatting to my neighbours, is there?'

'No, but I'm warning you now that you need to leave the investigating to us.' Her voice had a hard edge. He wondered who it was who'd gone complaining to the detective about him, and why she was so worked up about it.

'Of course, detective. I wouldn't dream of getting involved.' His voice was light and cheery. 'And now, don't let me keep you. I'm sure you've got lots of investigating to do. Let me know when you catch the vandal.'

He hung up and walked back to his car, whistling lightly. Ever since he'd been a child, plenty of people had tried to tell him what to do. He'd never been very good at listening to any of them. And he certainly wasn't planning to start now.

CHAPTER 6

That night, Jason dressed in a nice shirt and jeans and checked his reflection in his bedroom mirror. He wasn't vain – in fact, far from it. He usually didn't care at all what he looked like, as long as he was comfortable and didn't look like a hobo. But tonight, he was having dinner with two extremely important people. The most important people in the world to him, in fact. His kids, Jaxson and Inga.

He glanced in the mirror again. No spinach in his teeth, hair not sticking up. He really only cared because he didn't want to be one of these embarrassing dads wearing socks with sandals and T-shirts with daggy slogans on them. His reflection stared back at him – tall, over six foot two. Or 190 centimetres, to be exact, although he always thought of his height in feet. It was a habit picked up from reading too many American novels.

He ran a hand through his hair, which was starting to grey a bit at the temples, but he still had a full head of hair, unlike a few of his old classmates. He had fullback's shoulders, and although he didn't play rugby anymore, he could still pass for a player. Other than that, he was just a regular guy. Handsome enough in the right light, and still with the cheeky grin he'd had as a kid. He was probably never going to outgrow that. Good enough. He didn't have the pretty-boy looks of Tom Cruise or Ryan Gosling, but he wasn't going to embarrass his kids. And, if he turned on the charm, he could still do pretty well with the ladies. He'd take that any day of the week.

He was meeting the kids at the restaurant. One of the perks of having kids that were nearly grown up was that you didn't have to drive them around as much as you did when they were younger. Jason could remember years when it felt like he was always in the car, dropping them off and picking them up. Both kids were sporty, and it made for lots of after-school sports when they were kids. But tonight, Inga was getting a lift and Jax was driving himself. Jason shook his head at the thought. He could remember the day Jaxson was born as clearly as if it were yesterday, and now that same sweet child was old enough to drive a car. It seemed impossible. But still, he was incredibly proud of both kids. They'd grown into smart, hardworking, responsible adults – well, almost adults, anyway. Of all the things he'd achieved in his life, he was the proudest of them.

———

The restaurant was a small, dimly lit Mexican place in Golden Sands that Inga had suggested. Inside, on one wall there was a mural of women in traditional Mexican dress, dancing. Fairy lights were strung across the ceiling. The server led Jason to a table inlaid with colourful mosaic tiles, and he thought, *what the hell*, and ordered a margarita while he waited. Jax was the first to arrive. He was tall and slim, with a tennis player's strong arms and shoulders. Same cheeky smile as Jason's, but he had his mother's blue eyes. He was tanned from working outside, and it suited him.

'Hey, Jax!' Jason stood and gave him a big bear hug. 'How was work?' Jaxson was coaching tennis while he decided where he was going to university – hopefully somewhere with a good tennis program, because he had a gun serve and a killer backhand. Good enough to go pro with the right coaching, Jason thought. But, of course, he was biased when it came to his kids.

Jax shrugged. 'Yeah, pretty good. It's harder than you'd think, some days. You've really got to concentrate to spot the things clients need to work on. It can be pretty exhausting trying to keep them happy sometimes.'

He slid into the chair opposite Jason and ordered a drink just as Inga arrived. She was tall and blonde with a stunning smile, like his ex-wife, but Inga had green eyes instead of blue. She'd come straight from her job at a health food shop, one with quite a relaxed, casual vibe, so was wearing overalls with a rip in one knee, a multicoloured T-shirt and plaits in her hair.

'Dad! How great is this place? I told you it was good, didn't I?' Her enthusiasm was infectious. Jason gave her a huge hug and waved her into the seat next to Jax. By this time his margarita had arrived and he took a sip. It was good. Jax and Inny chatted back and forth for a few minutes about some kid they both knew. Jason wasn't really following the conversation, just watching his kids and thinking how great they'd both turned out. God, he was so proud of them. The waitress came, and Jason let Inga order for him. She was right, it really was a great restaurant. Maybe, if things went well with Mia, he'd bring her here.

'Did you watch that TikTok, Dad?' Inga asked. He was lost for a few minutes, before he worked out that a TikTok was a video of some sort, usually a person filming themself doing something funny. Inny pulled out her phone and showed him the screen. The young man in the video was doing impressions of the people you meet on a Sunshine Coast beach. The tourist, the surfer, the parents chasing their rowdy kids. It was pretty funny. He laughed loudly, which made Inga laugh too. Jason was the first to admit he was behind when it came to understanding technology, but he secretly loved it when his kids showed him all the silly and funny things they were into.

'So, how are things going with your project, Dad?' Jax asked between bites of the corn chips and guacamole the waiter had brought over.

Jason had never been good at hiding things from his kids, but he did his best. He didn't want to bring the mood down. 'Oh, you know, it's going pretty well. A few dramas this week, but hey. That's what you expect on a build site, right? Things can't go smoothly all the time.'

Both kids looked sceptical. They knew him well. 'What do you mean by dramas, Dad?' Inga asked with a frown. Jax just looked at him with the stare he knew well – he'd seen it in the mirror, the deadpan, silent stare he used whenever he felt like someone was holding out on him and he wanted them to tell him what was really going on. He usually used it on employees, but sometimes his kids. Obviously, Jax had picked up the habit.

He laughed. 'What is this, an interrogation? Nothing to worry about, really. Just some idiot vandalising the place.' He told them about the two different lots of damage to the site, and the two cryptic messages. He did his best to downplay it, shrugging and sipping at his drink. 'Probably just some bored kids trying to stir up trouble.'

Inga leaned forward in her chair, eyes wide. 'What if it's not, though? Maybe it's a clue to whoever is behind this. Maybe someone wants you to know it was them.'

He laughed. 'No, nothing like that, I'm sure. Plus the police are investigating already, so it's under control. I don't need to worry about trying to work out "whodunit".' That wasn't going to stop him from poking around and trying to find some answers himself, but he wasn't going to tell the kids that.

'It is weird though, isn't it?' Jax said. 'I mean, if it was just kids, why would they take the time to write messages like that? And what do they mean?'

Jason shrugged. 'It's nothing. Just kids trying to stir trouble.'

He paused for a moment, which was just long enough for Inga to read his face. She was always so good at doing that. He hated to admit it, but that came from her mother too. She looked at him quizzically, tilting her head. 'I reckon you've got a theory about it, haven't you Dad? What is it?'

He smiled. 'Not my theory, really. It's your Uncle Pauly's theory. He thinks both messages could have something to do with my childhood.' Both kids were leaning forward on the table now, ignoring the meals that had arrived as they were talking. He explained the theory, even though he wasn't convinced that it was right. 'It doesn't really make sense though, does it? I mean, who would know that kind of stuff about me?'

'Yeah, your childhood was kind of a long time ago,' Inny teased.

'Oi, you,' he shot a mock scowl in her direction. 'Behave!'

'Some people would know that stuff. Your brothers?' Jax asked.

Jason rolled his eyes. 'Nah. Not their style. They're not the subtle types. If one of them was pissed at me for some reason, they'd come and tell me to my face.'

Or try to deck me, he thought. Not that they'd succeed. He'd been ducking punches and serving them right back since they were all kids, brawling on the brown and orange carpet in Woodridge.

The kids turned back to their meals, out of ideas about what the cryptic clues might mean. That was fine. Jason was starting on his burritos, and they were really good. 'Just promise me, Dad, that when you find out more, you'll keep us posted, right?' Inga said.

He smiled. He'd do anything for his daughter. 'Of course I will.'

———

After both kids had gone – Inga to a friend's house, Jax to meet some mates who were going to see a band somewhere – Jason decided to walk around Golden Sands for a while. He thought about what Mia had said, about the place being different at night time. She was right. There was a different energy. He'd felt it the other night, walking through the streets with Pauly. It was the same now. A vibrant, pulsing energy, with restaurants crowded and music spilling from bars. He walked for a while, watching all the people out to have a good time. There were crowds of young people, wafting past in their figure-hugging dresses and skinny jeans, all laughing and talking loudly about some nonsense. There were tourists, young families pushing strollers and giving toddlers shoulder rides, couples on dates. He wandered aimlessly, happy just to people-watch and enjoy the warm night air. But eventually, he made his way back toward the build site. It pulled at him like a magnet.

At this time of night, the whole site was dark. The security fence stood like a ring of sentries around the property, and even though he couldn't see them, he knew the new cameras were recording any movement. He should smile for the camera. He didn't, though.

Instead, he stood still, listening for anything that sounded out of the ordinary. Not that anything seemed to be moving in the area. He could hear distant, pumping bass coming from the direction of the Galaxy. Although the neon sign was blinking brightly, the place still seemed deserted. Too early, he guessed, although he had a feeling that business at the Galaxy was always slow.

Across the road from the build site was a Thai restaurant called Golden Basil. At this time of the evening, it looked as though trade there was starting to slow. There were only a few customers inside, still eating. Jason snagged a table out the front and ordered a drink. Just a soda water. He watched the build site for a while, thinking about the vandalism. He could still picture the dripping red letters. *Pride goes before a fall. Watch out you don't fall and break your head.* Maybe Pauly was right and that message was somehow related to the incident from his childhood. He let his mind wander, right back to that day, all those years ago.

———

The apartment had belonged to his aunty. If he closed his eyes, he could still picture the inside of it. Cluttered with all kinds of knick-knacks, kids toys and china ornaments. It smelled like lavender and soap, and there were those little lace doilies on pretty much every available surface. On that particular day the apartment had also been full of kids. He and his brothers and cousins had all played and fought inside as usual. They'd been hyped up on red cordial and chased each other from room to room. Mum and Aunty Sue were both sitting at the kitchen table, drinking cups of tea. He'd climbed up onto the back of a couch, out of reach of one of his little cousins who was trying to wrestle him. The cousin got distracted and darted off to attack one of his brothers, but Jason stayed up on the back of the couch. In a rare quiet moment, he'd been watching the chaos in the room, an observer rather than the ringleader he usually was. Always a mistake to stay still too long but there it was – he'd been watching the other kids, waiting for his opportunity to dive back into the action.

For just a moment, he'd leaned back against the flywire of the window behind him. He hadn't even registered there was a window there. And then, with a pop, it had given way. There was nothing behind him but the air. He tumbled backward before he'd had time to react, grab onto the couch or a curtain, anything to stop his fall. And then – he could still remember it like it was yesterday – that moment when it seemed like he was suspended in midair, his mouth frozen in an O of surprise, his arms reaching back toward the window. The moment stretched out like warm toffee, and the next instant he was lying on his back on the ground, stunned.

It seemed as though the world had stopped moving and he'd become part of the wide blue sky that extended overhead. For a moment, the only sound he could hear was the ringing in his ears. In the distance, up at the window he had come from, the flywire was hanging loose in the breeze and a row of shocked faces was peering from the window. Then he could hear his mother's scream and the babble of the neighbourhood kids. The faces disappeared from the window and he heard a door slam in the distance, the sound of faraway voices. He felt like he should get up, but he couldn't seem to catch his breath. All the wind had been knocked out of him. And then a little knot of kids formed around him. Most of them were kids he knew. Mitch. Thommo. Richie, the kid whose parents owned the pool. Pauly, who had recently moved into the neighbourhood. After only a couple of weeks they were already best mates, upsetting the previous pecking order of who hung around with who. His mum pushed the kids aside, and he could hear her voice over the murmur of the kids and his still-ringing ears. 'Stay still, Jason. Don't get up. Your back could be hurt.'

He wanted to tell her that his back was fine, but he'd somehow forgotten how to breathe. The words wouldn't come.

'He didn't land on his back,' one of the kids said. Richie, maybe, or Thommo. 'He landed on his head. Only just missed that concrete bit.' The kid pointed to a flower bed with a thick concrete border just beyond his head.

He could see the fear in his mother's face then and tried to reassure her as soon as he could suck in a breath of air. 'I'm okay, Mum, really.

Just winded.' But all the same, he stayed still. For some reason, he couldn't seem to make his eyes focus.

And he had been fine, despite his mothers' fears. The doctor proclaimed he had a concussion. He'd spent a couple of nights in hospital, where he'd fallen madly in love with a pretty nurse who'd given him extra jelly and custard. He'd been allowed to watch as much TV as he wanted, and he'd discovered that one of the channels showed Jerry Springer at lunchtimes. He saved up all the stories about guys cheating on their girlfriends with the girlfriends' sisters, and the woman who claimed to be married to a horse, to tell to his friends back at school. Then he tried to convince the pretty nurse – her name was Nina, maybe, or Rita, he couldn't remember now – that he was actually older than he looked. It hadn't been that bad at all.

———

He drew his mind back from the memory and watched the silent, dark construction site. The air was still balmy and chatter from people on the street washed over him like waves. It was stupid to think the graffiti had anything to do with that incident. It was just a coincidence. The only problem was, Jason didn't really believe in coincidences.

He finished the last of his drink and paid. He thought about asking the waitstaff some questions, but they all seemed busy and he was ready to go home. He'd ask questions another night. He walked back up the street toward the car park near the Mexican restaurant where he'd parked earlier that night. He glanced at the Galaxy as he walked past, but it still looked deserted, just a bored-looking bouncer picking his teeth outside the front door. As he walked on, a figure approached, hurrying down the footpath. It was a girl, he guessed, wearing a black jumper with the hood pulled over her head.

As he passed her, the girl looked up, and he recognised her. Stella. She had the same mouse-frightened look she'd had that night when he'd seen her at the Galaxy. Why was she going back there? He watched as she glanced around. For a moment their eyes met, and he could see the flash of recognition on her face. He thought about stopping her and asking if she was okay, but she quickly looked away from him, and he recognised the emotion that flickered over her face before she hurried past. Fear. The same scared look that had been on her face in the club that night. She wasn't scared of him, he was sure. But she was definitely scared of something. Probably that asshole guy who'd been threatening her. He glanced around, making sure no-one was following her. Then he turned back to the girl, all of his protective instincts kicking in. But she was already gone.

CHAPTER 7

The next morning Jason was at the build site, coffee in hand, before the shops opposite had even opened their doors. The gate in the security fence was open and there were delivery vans and work utes parked in the driveway. Tradies were wandering around, some drinking iced coffees or eating breakfast, some smoking idly at the back of the building before they got started for the day. He was grateful to see that everything seemed normal. Nothing out of place. Still, to be sure, he went inside to check.

He walked through the shell of the building, already seeing in his mind's eye the luxury apartment that would fill the space that for now was bare concrete and unfinished stud walls. He wandered through the bare rooms, electrical cables sprouting from the walls here and there, through to where the sabotage had taken place the day before. The chippies had repaired most of the broken studwork from the day before, but he could still see some chunks out of the concrete where someone had swung a hammer in some kind of frenzy. On the walls, the red paint still dripped its cryptic message. Jason frowned, wondering if there was some kind of meaning to it he was missing. Surely it couldn't have anything to do with a little incident from his childhood, could it?

He chased the thought from his mind and carried on through the site, admiring the progress that had been made in the last few days. He wandered back toward the entrance, where the various tradies were picking up tools and putting on their hi-vis. He could hear them chatting to each other, clanking their tool belts and stomping the dust off their boots. Frank came around the corner, clipboard in hand.

'Oh. There you are, boss.'

'How's it going, Frank? Everything going according to plan?'

Frank nodded. As always, he was a man of few words. 'Yep. No problems, if you don't count that damage yesterday. The lads have cleaned most of it up, and I'll get one of the apprentices to paint over that red shit on the wall today.'

'Right. That's great, Frank. And the security cameras are up? No problems there?'

Frank's eyes darted upwards, and Jason followed his glance. Up in the corner, barely visible unless you knew what you were looking for, was a tiny electronic dome. One of the cameras.

'Yeah, they're up. I guess they're working. I don't know. The video gets sent straight to the office, right?'

Jason nodded. He'd get Rachel to check on her end, but it looked like the cameras were up, and hopefully operational. 'That's great, Frank. Thanks for helping with that.'

'Righto. Well, I'd better get back to it. Get this lot moving,' said Frank. He pointed over his shoulder to where a few men in work boots and hard hats were milling around waiting for instructions. And a few women, Jason noticed. Construction was still a fairly male-dominated field, but there were a few more women joining the trades these days, and Jason liked to make sure he gave them every opportunity he could. Made sure that Frank and the other supervisors kept the workplace free from the kinds of harassment and sexism that he knew some female tradies faced in other workplaces. Of course, it was always going to be a pretty blokey environment, but he liked to think if his daughter had ever thought about going into construction, she wouldn't have to face the kind of rubbish that women had had to put up with in the past.

Frank turned and barked out a few instructions to the guys

standing behind him. It didn't take much, just a few words here and there, just a few questions answered. Then he turned back to Jason. 'Right boss? I've got to go out the back, make sure the right plumbing stuff has turned up this time.'

Jason nodded. He thought about telling Frank, for the hundredth time, not to call him boss but decided not to. Wasn't worth wasting his time. Frank hadn't listened to him the first hundred times, wasn't likely to listen this time either. Jason didn't like being called boss – he knew what it was like on a building site, and he knew that although you had to have someone calling the shots and paying the bills, every single person was important, right down to the newest apprentice. But some habits were deeply ingrained, especially when it came to old chippies like Frank.

He walked around to the front of the site, checking progress on a few key areas as he went. The scaffolding was going up at the front of the building, and the cladding on the façade would be up soon. It would change the look of the front entirely, making it look less like a generic concrete behemoth and more like the unique, luxury building it was going to be. He was excited. They were making good progress, and the vandalism hadn't slowed them down too much. He thought about Brian's project just a couple of streets away, and wondered if he'd had any delays. They'd been friends, once. Why not pop in and see how his project was going?

———

From the outside, Brian's build site was surprisingly similar to Jason's. Same kind of security fence, same bare grey concrete facade waiting to be made into something beautiful. The street the project was on was one closer to the beach, always a huge drawcard, but the site was further away from the centre of Golden Sands. Here, there were office buildings and parking lots, rather than the chic wine bars, coffee shops and upmarket delis that surrounded Jason's site. There were pros and cons to both sites, of course, but if Jason had to choose, he'd pick his own site every time.

Jason walked up to the gate in the security fencing and was met by a bored guy in high-vis and work boots wielding a clipboard. A security guard. That was something he didn't have on his site. Perhaps Brian had had some issues with vandalism as well? Jason thought for a moment that he might need to employ a security guy for his own build site. Maybe that would stop the problems? He dismissed the thought. The vandalism was happening at night, not during the day, and what could possibly happen on the site when it was swarming with builders, plumbers, concreters, electricians, plasterers, carpenters and apprentices? Not to mention the foremen, delivery drivers, architects, tilers, painters and cabinetmakers. He smiled to himself, and decided that having a security guy posted at the front gate would definitely be overkill.

'Name?' the bored guy with the clipboard asked him.

'Gus Stubbs,' Jason answered. It had been a silly in-joke with his mates back in high school, each competing to give themselves the funniest fake names. And although he and Brian weren't really mates anymore, sometimes old habits die hard.

The security guy wrote down his name on the list without so much as a chuckle. Then he looked up from the clipboard. 'What's the reason for visiting the site today, Mr Stubbs?'

'I'm here to see Brian. We're old mates. Is he here?'

Bored clipboard guy nodded, making a note on the clipboard. 'Yep, here somewhere. Go in that direction, and you'll hear him. He's sure to be shouting at someone.'

Jason smiled. Brian was notorious for having a short fuse. He was glad he wasn't a tradie on this site. He motioned thanks to the security guy and walked in, following the sounds of machinery around to the back of the site. Here, too, the similarities with his site continued. The place was a hive of activity, various people buzzing around wearing hard hats. Jason stopped a young guy who was carrying a nail gun. 'Is Brian around, mate?'

'Yeah. The old bastard's back that way,' he grumbled, his thumb gesturing toward the back of the site. Jason followed the directions until he found a knot of men standing around sulkily while Brian shouted at them. He gathered that someone had made a mistake with the concreting, and now a section of it had to be pulled out and redone.

Jason smiled to himself. That was Brian. He always did things in a half-assed way and then blamed other people when things went wrong. Back when they'd been working together, Brian had regularly cut the decking planks the wrong length but he never took responsibility for his own mistakes. It was always someone else's fault. Mistakes happened, that was fine, but Jason was a big believer in owning your stuff-ups.

When Brian's tirade had finished, Jason stepped over to where he was scowling at some architect's plans. Brian was about the same age as he was but he hadn't aged very gracefully. He was balding and had started to develop a beer belly. Plus, his forehead was lined with the permanent lines of someone who was perpetually in a bad mood.

'Brian, mate, how are ya? Got some problems with the plans?'

Brian looked up and frowned. 'Jason. It's been a while. No, no problems, everything's going well here. How about you? Come to steal some of my ideas?'

Jason laughed. 'Oh, if only they were worth stealing, man.' He looked around. 'How's it all going? Looks like you're making some progress.'

Brian snorted. 'Plenty of progress. We're on schedule, all going well.' He gave Jason a shrewd look. 'How about you? I hear you've had some trouble?'

Jason raised an eyebrow. 'Yeah? Where'd you hear that?'

Brian glanced away. 'Oh, you know. You hear things from the workers. Can't really remember where I heard it. On the grapevine.' He waved a hand dismissively.

'What have you heard?'

Brian frowned. 'Someone's got it in for you, right? Been damaging your site. You must have got on someone's nerves.' He gave Jason an oily smile.

Jason shrugged. 'Yeah. Just kids playing pranks, right? Stupid, juvenile stuff. It hasn't stopped our progress.' He scowled and took a step toward Brian, leaning over him. Brian was a good twenty centimetres shorter than him. Jason had a good twenty kilos or so on him too, despite Brian's beer belly. He could see the other man's eyes widen with sudden fear. Good. That meant he was paying attention. He didn't think Brian had anything to do with the damage but it didn't hurt to send a message. 'But, if it happens again, it's going to really piss me off. I'll find who's behind it and make them pay.'

Brian took a step backward, away from Jason, his eyes darting around. 'Yeah, yeah, sure mate. I ah, I don't know anything about it, but if I hear anything, I'll be sure to let you know, right?'

Jason relaxed his threatening posture and smiled. 'I'd appreciate it. Thanks, mate.'

'So, is there anything else I can help you with?' Brian asked, his eyes still wide.

'Nah, not at all. Just came by to say hello and see how you were getting on.' Jason smiled. 'It's looking good, mate. A long way up from installing backyard decking, isn't it? We've both done well for ourselves.'

And with that, he clapped Brian on the shoulder, turned and walked away.

———

Later that afternoon, Jason found himself in a booth in a comfortable little coffee shop, sitting across from Mia. He'd asked her to show him the best place for coffee in Golden Sands, half expecting she'd take him to a hipster place with milk crates for seats and staff wearing ripped skinny jeans and an air of haughty superiority. But instead, she'd arranged to meet him at Tony's, an unpretentious little cafe on a side street near his building site.

The little melamine tables and red vinyl upholstery in the booths didn't inspire much confidence, and neither did the man behind the coffee machine, who must have been pushing seventy at least, but he trusted Mia so had ordered a latte and a slice of the sponge cake in the cabinet before sliding into the booth opposite her. She was even more gorgeous than he'd remembered. Up close, he could see the tiny sprinkle of freckles across her nose and the glossy sheen of her hair. She smelled sweet, like vanilla cookies and something floral that Jason couldn't quite place.

'See the old guy making our coffees?' Mia asked.

'Yeah. Normally I don't trust anyone over the age of twenty-five to make a decent coffee.'

She laughed. 'Well, that's Tony, the owner. He's been making coffee since before either of us was born. His wife makes the cakes. Trust me. The place might not be fancy, but they're the best.'

Jason looked around. The little shop was fairly full, and there was a steady stream of customers coming in for takeaway coffee as well. A young waiter brought over a tray with their coffees and Jason's cake.

'Normally I wouldn't eat cake unless it's a special occasion, right. But I just can't pass up sponge cake. Plus, going out for coffee with you is a special occasion.' He spooned a bite of the cake into his mouth and groaned with pleasure. 'This is just like what my Nan Dooksie makes. Light and fluffy, with strawberries in the cream. Here, you've got to try some.'

He pushed the plate over toward her, and she took a spoonful. Before long, the whole generous slice of cake had disappeared, shared between the two of them. The coffee lived up to Mia's description too, and they laughed and chatted as they ate.

'Well, Mia, you were right. This place is the best. Good call.' He leaned back in his seat.

'I do take my coffee seriously. Just about as seriously as you take your cake,' she teased.

Jason laughed and leaned in toward her. 'So, tell me about you, Mia.' She started to talk and he watched her, always content to admire a beautiful woman. Mia had an unselfconscious air about her, as though she was entirely comfortable in her own skin. She told him about growing up in Melbourne, the youngest child in a big family, before deciding to move north for the warmer weather. 'I hated winters growing up. Every autumn I'd start to get depressed as the days got colder. I'm really much more comfortable in the heat,' she laughed.

He talked about growing up in Woodridge, about starting out building decks and slowly working his way up to where he was now. His biggest project yet. He told her about his kids, and how wonderful they were. When Mia eventually looked at her watch and said she needed to be getting back to the office, Jason wasn't sure if they'd been talking for a few hours or mere minutes. He was very sure he wanted to spend more time with her, though.

'I'm sorry, Jason, but I'm going to disappoint you,' she said. 'I haven't been able to find out who owns the Galaxy Nightclub yet. I'm still working on it.'

He laughed. 'I'm not disappointed. In fact, that's good. It gives me another reason to catch up with you again.'

She winked at him. 'Maybe that's why I'm taking my time with it.'

They waved to Tony as they headed toward the door, and Jason swore he'd be back again soon. The best coffee he'd had in a while, and sponge cake just like his nan used to make.

'I forgot to ask,' Mia said as they walked out onto the street. 'How's everything going with your project? No more issues?'

Jason smiled. 'No, no more issues. It was just kids playing pranks. I'm sure it won't happen again.'

CHAPTER 8

ason was on the beach when his phone rang. The sharp noise shattered the peace of the early morning solitude. He'd been watching the rays of sunlight play on the surface of the water, and enjoying the quiet. Of course, the beach wasn't entirely quiet. There was the persistent rhythm of the waves on the sand, the dog barking in the distance, and the cheery calls of the early morning walkers. But it was different to the usual urban noises of a city, and he found the stillness a perfect way to focus his mind. Until his phone rang.

'Hey boss,' Frank's voice sounded urgent down the phone line. 'You'd better come in. There's something you need to take a look at.'

Jason frowned. 'More vandalism?'

'Yeah. Just… maybe you should come in.'

'Right. I'll head straight there. Can you keep it contained for the moment?'

'I'll do my best.' Frank rang off.

Jason took one more look at the serene beach scene, glad he'd been able to start the day with a bit of tranquillity. Then he turned away, ready to face the new challenge. Shit. He'd had enough of this rubbish already.

When he got to the build site, he pulled up in a nearby carpark. A small group of people was gathered near the site, which was unusual for that time of morning. Jason threaded his way through the little crowd and saw what had attracted them there. Some of the scaffolding at the front of his building was hanging loosely, pulled apart from its supports and threatening to fall at any moment. It was inside the security fence, but because of its height, the metal parts would fall onto the footpath if it came down. Behind the crooked poles and platforms, Jason could see a scrawl on the front of the concrete building, in red paint. He couldn't make out what it was. It was certainly attracting attention though. The people milling around were pointing up at it and speaking in low tones to each other.

Closer to the entrance, Frank was shouting directions at two workers who were trying to manoeuvre a scissor lift into the small gap between the scaffold and the security fence. The damaged scaffolding needed to be taken down before it fell down. Jason could see the scissor lift wasn't going to be high enough, though, and it was going to take too long. He stepped to the front of the people scattered across the road and footpath in front of the building and began urging people to move backward. They were too busy gawking to see the danger.

He put on his best crowd-control voice. 'Come on folks, move back please. It's not safe.'

They grumbled, but did as he asked, moving to the side of the footpath, or over the road. Just in time. A gust of wind caught the swinging bits of metal and pushed them to the side, enough to overbalance the whole structure. Jason looked up from the people shuffling backward, just in time to see a whole section of the scaffolding tear loose with a screech. Metal crashed down onto the footpath that Jason had just cleared, narrowly missing someone's car. There were gasps and shrieks of alarm from the assembled people, and some particularly choice swear words from Frank. A car alarm started up as well, adding to the mayhem. Then, after the sound of crashing metal had subsided, there was a moment of quiet, punctuated by the beeping of the alarm. Jason looked up and read the words painted across the front of the building in dripping, blood-red paint. *You think you're cool, surfer man? Waves, cars, you'll crash down in the end.* For a moment, Jason felt his hair stand on end.

The murmuring of people on the footpath, pointing at the painted words, looking around with puzzled faces, was interrupted by a siren. Two police cars screeched to a halt in front of the site. Detective Riggs got out of the first one, followed by a few more officers in uniform. Jason walked over to greet them, his jaw clenched tight.

'Morning, Riggs,' he called.

'What's going on here?' she asked in a brusque tone, interrupting his friendly greeting.

Jason's smile was tight. 'Oh, you know. Early morning yoga session. This is where we like to do our yoga, right here on the footpath. Going to join us?'

She glared at him. 'Is this a joke to you?'

'No, of course not,' he fired back at her. 'But saying good morning doesn't take much time out of your busy day, does it detective?'

She didn't apologise, but she did drop the frown. Jason would get her to smile one of these days, he decided. 'More vandalism?'

Jason nodded. 'Yeah. My foreman rang me early this morning. Looks like they've targeted the scaffolding and the front of the building.' He looked up to see Frank approaching. 'Here he is now.'

Riggs looked at Frank. 'You were first on site this morning?'

'Yeah.' Frank took off his hard hat and rubbed the back of his hand across his forehead. 'Found the scaffolding hanging loose. And the paint.' He waved a hand toward the dripping letters. 'There's a bit more damage inside too, but not much.'

'We got some security cameras put in after the last attack,' Jason said. 'We should be able to see who it was this time.'

'They did this as well?' Riggs nodded at the twisted metal across the footpath. She looked up at the gap in the scaffolding. Around her, two other police officers were putting up tape to keep the area clear. Another was taking statements from some of the spectators who were still watching from the other side of the road. Jason noticed that a lot of the crowd had dispersed, melting away as soon as the police cars arrived.

'Yeah,' Frank looked at the scaffolding. 'It was damaged when I got here. Fell down just before you arrived.'

Riggs had pulled out a notebook and was writing in it. 'And the security fence was still locked when you got here?'

Frank nodded. 'Yep. I opened it.'

The three of them looked at the fence. It was tall, made from strong mesh. It would be difficult to climb, Jason thought, but not impossible. 'So must have been someone fit and agile,' Riggs noted. 'Like we thought, maybe some bored teenagers.'

'Actually, I'm not so sure about that now,' Jason said. 'It's not so easy to pull that scaffolding apart like that. You'd need to have tools. It's bolted together. I mean, I haven't had a really good look at it, but my guess is whoever damaged the scaffold knew what they were doing. Maybe someone who'd worked with scaffolding before? Someone with a bit of know-how, anyway.'

Riggs looked at him and raised her eyebrows. She made a note in her book. Jason glanced at Frank, too, who was wide-eyed. Perhaps he was thinking about the different crew members they'd had on site who had experience with scaffolding. There were a lot of them – it wasn't an uncommon job for tradies to do. You needed a couple of tickets, particularly if you were going to work past a certain height, but they didn't take too long to get.

'So, maybe it wasn't teenagers,' Riggs said. 'But maybe someone who's experienced with building.' She gave Jason a sidelong glance. 'Like I said, it could be an inside job. One of your workers with a grudge against you for some reason. It happens.'

Jason shrugged. 'I doubt it. I mean, I don't know everyone on the site. We hire in a lot of contractors for things like plumbing, electrics, painting, that kind of thing. And sometimes we'll hire new tradies, new apprentices.' He looked at Frank. 'But like I told you before, we've done a few jobs with this crew now, and they're all pretty solid. I'd trust them all.'

Frank nodded his agreement, but there was something in his face that Jason couldn't read. Jason made a mental note to ask him about it later when Riggs wasn't around. Maybe Frank had his suspicions about some of the crew.

Riggs made a few more notes in her book. 'Well, we'll ask around and see if anyone has seen anything. And we're going to need that security camera footage, of course.' She looked up at the red paint on the building. 'How about that message? *You think you're cool, surfer man?*' she read. '*Waves, cars, you'll crash down in the end.* That's a really weird message. I guess you're going to tell me it doesn't mean anything to you, Jason? Nothing to do with you? Just some cryptic crap?' She raised her eyebrows at him, sceptical.

Jason shook his head. 'Not this time. This time I think I know exactly what it means. And yeah, it's personal. I'm pretty sure that message is directed at me, by someone who has known me for a long time.'

Riggs raised her expressive eyebrows. 'Right. And I suppose you're going to tell me you know who that is?'

He wished he did. 'No. Still no clue.'

'Right. Well, as soon as we've secured the scene, you can explain.'

The police officers went about their jobs and Frank headed off to talk to the crew members who were starting to straggle in. But Jason needed a few minutes to clear his mind. He put his hands in his pockets, walking away from the site and through the streets in the direction of the beach, his mind swirling with the cryptic message on the side of the building. He needed to think. He squeezed his eyes shut, just for a moment, and the memories came flooding over him.

———

It started out as one of those perfect summer evenings on the Goldie. The night air was cool after the oppressive heat of the day, and everywhere he looked there were people. They strolled down the sidewalks, the women sleek and beautiful in short skirts and high heels. There were businessmen in crisp pants and short-sleeved shirts, ties loosened, and tourists wearing cargo shorts, loud shirts and sunburn. There were families, the children tired and happy, full of fish and chips, smeared with ice cream. Older couples, too, strolling hand in hand, out for a quiet dinner. Cars drove past, windows rolled down, the thump of bass-heavy music rising and falling as they passed.

Jason let the noise and the bustle spin around him. He walked through the crowds on the street, unhurried. He was lean and hard-muscled from a summer spent surfing and playing rugby. Tanned from days spent at the beach, lying on beach towels next to girls in bikinis, flirting and laughing. At the restaurant, some of the boys were waiting, already seated at a long table. They spotted him at the door and stood, crowding around him. They all patted each other on the backs, shaking hands and calling each other by their nicknames. It felt like old times, when they were at school together or running wild on the weekends.

They ate burgers and drank pints of cold beer, telling stories and tall tales about what they'd been doing since they were all together. Jason told them about working as a surf instructor, and a groan of jealousy rolled around the table. He was getting paid to surf. The rest of them bemoaned their jobs shelving groceries or labouring on building sites. He laughed at them, told them he'd recommend one of them for the job when he quits. Who wants it most? By then, he was getting bored with it, to tell the truth.

The job was great for meeting girls. More days than he could remember, he'd taken one of them back to the van, and they'd had slow, languid sex on the mattress in the back, surrounded by surfboards. He could taste the sea salt on their lips. The smell of surfboard wax hung in the air around them, mixed with the coconut smell of Reef suntan oil. He'd forgotten their names, mostly. Rebecca. Tina. Lucy. Missy. He'd been a little bit in love with each of them. But still, as far as the job went, it didn't challenge him. He had bigger ideas, bigger plans. He laughed, and told the boys that whoever bought him drinks for the night could take the job off his hands. 'More girls than you can imagine,' he told them. 'They'll throw themselves at you.'

The boys joked and teased, and he counted himself lucky to be back with them. The Wolf Pack. They called themselves that, ironically, but he knew each one of them would be there for him if he ever needed a mate. These were the kinds of friendships that would last them a lifetime. When they're older, he knew, with kids and families of their own, they'd still be meeting for drinks, still teasing each other over the same stupid shit they did as kids. They'd still have each other's backs. He felt warm at the thought, then laughed at his own sentimentality.

He drained the last of his beer. 'Come on, let's get out of here, fellas. The night is young. Let's go to a club.'

Around the table there were nods of agreement. A few of the boys shook their heads, claiming early starts in the morning, and the rest of them teased and laughed. In the end, only a couple were left, shaking hands all round and making plans to catch up again soon. They swaggered down the street to the club they all liked best, just a few blocks away. It was still early enough that there weren't long lines at the door, and the bouncer saw them coming. A group of good-looking young men, well dressed, wallets no doubt full from summer jobs or rich parents. He checked IDs, barely looking at them, and waved them through. By then, they were all old enough to get in legally. Jason remembered the days of fake IDs, of having to remember unfamiliar birthdates, the little adrenaline rush of being able to fool the bouncer into thinking you were older. A little part of him missed the challenge. He always got in. Even when his friends were turned away.

Inside the music was loud and the bass echoed in his chest. The dance floor was full and he could feel the pull of the music. The boys milled around, nudging him, pointing out a blonde girl in a tight blue dress. He smiled at her, and she winked. It was a challenge, but one that could wait. First, he wanted to get onto the dance floor, to get lost in the music. One of the boys thrust a drink into his hand. Jason laughed. 'You must really want that job, hey Willo?' He gulped it back and pushed through the growing crowd to the dance floor. The music swelled and pulsed around him, pumping through his body. He was lost in it, lost in the rhythm, feeling the push and heat of bodies all around him. The music filled his mind, until there was no room for anything else.

Later, they spilled back out of the club and into the night air. By this time it was darker, and there were fewer people on the streets. Still, the air felt full of an electric buzz, an energy that pulsed and swelled around them. Jason could feel the booze and the adrenaline in his bloodstream. On a usual night out, he would take it as a challenge to get a girl to go home with him. Not tonight though – it had been far too long since he'd had a night out with the boys, and tonight he wanted to enjoy their company. He had the blonde girl's phone number written on a serviette in his pocket, though.

There were only a few of them by this time, just a handful of the main crew, the rest fading away one by one to go home to jobs or girl-friends or curfews. They walked to Willo's car. He'd stopped drinking a few hours back, he said, and offered to drive them home. Getting responsible. They were getting old. What a thought, when they'd been just on the cusp of adulthood, barely more than teenagers. Willo's car was a Volvo station wagon, his mum's car, and they laughed and teased him. They told him they wouldn't be seen dead in that piece of shit, they'd rather walk, and he protested, weakly. But still, there were no taxis around and besides, they'd spent all their money. The edges of the night sky were already starting to lighten. They piled in, too many broad shoulders in a confined space. Jason hung back, though.

'Start it up, Willo. I'll ride on top,' he shouted through the open window. His mates shouted back, laughing at him. It was not the first time he'd done it, and he could feel the rush already starting to over-ride the alcohol in his veins. Willo started the car, and Jason shouted and jumped, pulling himself onto his stomach on the roof of the car. The booze fuzzed the edges of his vision, but he was on. It was like riding a wave, the cold wind in his face, all of his muscles tense as he balanced against the forces that wanted to pull him to the ground. Willo was speeding up now, all the boys hanging out the open windows and shouting at him. He couldn't make out the words, but he knew they were shouting encouragement. He stood, knees bent, feeling the wind rush in his face. Falling would mean death, or at least serious injury. But he was invincible. He was a Leo, born in the year of the tiger, so he had eighteen lives. Up here, standing on the moving car, he knew he needed every one of those lives. But he knew he wouldn't fall.

Willo took a corner, and some pedestrians shouted in surprise, seeing him on the roof. He slipped, nearly lost his footing, and another burst jof adrenaline shot through him. Then he was up again, watching the blur of lights as they went past. The car sped up, and all his nerve endings were alive with the thrill of it. In the distance he saw the red and blue flash of police lights, and Willo took the next corner in the opposite direction. It didn't matter, though, because nothing could touch him. Nothing could stop him. In that moment, he was sure that he would live forever. Nothing mattered except for the wind in his face and the forces that pushed against him as he balanced, as he stood. He tipped his head back, watching the sprinkle of stars in the velvet sky. He breathed deep, willing the moment to go on forever.

CHAPTER 9

ason's phone rang, pulling him away from his memories. He glanced down at the screen. An unknown number. He almost decided not to answer it, but changed his mind. It was, as he'd guessed, Detective Riggs.

'Jason? Have you left the site?' she asked. 'We need to talk to you again.'

'Yeah, I just went for a walk. Needed to clear my head.'

'Well, can you come back here?' She sounded irritated, but he guessed that was about usual for the detective.

'Sure,' he said, in a cheery voice that took a bit of effort. 'I'll see you in a few minutes.' He hung up and slipped the phone back into his pocket. He strolled back in the direction of the building site, taking his time. He couldn't care less that the detective was annoyed. He thought about stopping to get a coffee but decided against it. He'd get one later, at that little cafe that Mia had taken him to.

On the way back to the site Jason thought about the cryptic message that had been painted on the wall. Was he jumping to conclusions by thinking that the message referred to his car surfing days? Who would know about him doing that? Only a handful of his friends who'd been around in those days. Pauly, of course, and some of the guys from school. He didn't see many of them anymore. He thought back, trying to remember who he might have told about those wild and stupid days when he seemed immune from any kind of danger. He'd probably told a few people over the years. His brothers, for example. But not that many. He knew what most people would think of that kind of behaviour – reckless and dangerous. And he certainly hadn't told anyone in the last five years or so. As his kids had reached their teens, he'd suddenly been gripped with fear that they might try something stupid like that. They were both sensible, responsible kids, though, which sometimes surprised him when he thought they were carrying half his DNA. At their age, he'd been irresponsible. Fearless.

There was no point trying to decipher the message, he realised. He'd drive himself mad trying to do that. Better to just catch the bastard who was messing up his site, then he could get the information out of him directly. Much more direct. Jason hated beating around the bush. He wasn't interested in mind games or trying to second-guess what someone meant. He tried to be straightforward and honest, and he liked it when people were that way with him, too.

Back at the site, Riggs was standing on the front footpath, waiting for him. He smiled as he approached, sure that would add just a little to her irritation. Which wasn't his problem.

'How can I help you, detective?' he asked.

'Jason. I've been speaking to my superiors, and we're going to have to shut your site down for a while. A member of the public could have been harmed this morning. We can't allow that to happen again.'

'Hey, woah, wait a minute,' Jason said, holding up his hands. 'So, you're telling me, not only am I facing increasing costs and delays from this vandalism, you're also going to hold me up even further?'

'Yes, but I'm sure you understand. There's a risk to the public…'

'And not only that,' he interrupted her, 'but so far you haven't managed to catch whoever is doing this. Haven't got a single lead that I can tell.' Now *he* was annoyed.

'We're working on that,' she said stiffly. 'But in the meantime, in the interests of public safety, we're going to shut down this site.'

'No. No way.' He didn't raise his voice, but his tone was like steel. 'Who is your superior? I'll talk to them directly.'

Riggs rolled her eyes. 'You can't do that. Besides, there's a risk to public…'

He interrupted her again, his voice still steel. 'Oh, believe me. I can. I'll put on more security but you are not shutting down this site. Now tell me, who is your superior?'

———

Riggs grumbled and huffed about it, but the site was not shut down. Jason agreed to hire a security firm to do periodic checks throughout the night, which he'd been thinking of doing anyway, and Frank got the crew back to work.

'Frank, as soon as the scaffolding is fixed, can you get someone up there to paint over that stupid message on the front wall?' Jason asked. Every time he looked at the red letters, he felt a rising anger. Frank nodded and ambled off to get started. Jason could feel an itching determination to get to the bottom of the whole mystery. By now he was well and truly annoyed at the interruptions to his project, and he was going to make someone pay for it.

Despite his growing conviction the vandal must be someone with a personal vendetta against him, someone with quite a detailed knowledge of his past, he didn't have a clue who it could be. He didn't want to waste his time going through his memory, trying to think of who might have known about the car surfing and who might be holding a grudge against him. And fortunately, he wouldn't have to. With any luck, the security camera footage would show exactly who the culprit was. He turned toward his car and ran right into Detective Riggs.

'Do you need anything else here, Detective Riggs? I'm heading off.'

Riggs nodded. 'Yes. We're going to need access to your security cameras.'

'Of course. I'm going to go and take a look at the footage now. I'll bring it to you when I'm done.' Well, probably Rachel would email it or something. He wasn't sure, and he didn't care.

Riggs shook her head. 'No, I'm afraid I'm going to need it first, before you look at it.'

Jason frowned. 'I don't think so. They're my security cameras. I'm not going to just hand the footage over to you. I'm going to look at it first.'

Riggs sighed. 'What, so you can take some vigilante action against whoever damaged your property? I don't think so.'

That was exactly what Jason was planning, not that he'd admit it to a police officer. 'I won't do anything stupid, detective. But I've got the right to see my own security camera footage, haven't I?'

She sighed again, theatrically. Maybe she'd missed her calling and should have been an actor. 'Jason, we have to take into account every possibility. And one possibility is that you are the one who is damaging the site.'

'What? Are you serious? Why the hell would I damage my own building site?'

She shrugged. 'I don't know. Insurance money? Maybe things aren't going well and you're trying to cover up shoddy work? I have no idea. Chances are it's not you, but we have to consider it as a possibility. So, I need to get that footage before you watch it. We can do it the easy way or the hard way, which will mean me getting a warrant, but I'd prefer to do it the easy way.'

Once again, Jason shook his head. 'I'm not going to just hand it over without even looking at the footage myself. And besides, maybe I'll be able to identify the perpetrator. It's probably someone I know, right?'

Detective Riggs folded her arms across her chest. For a moment, Jason thought she was going to keep arguing. Instead, she nodded. 'Alright. You can come with us and we'll look at the footage together. That way you get to satisfy your curiosity and I get to make sure you're not deleting anything incriminating.'

'Deal. Not that there's anything incriminating on there,' Jason said.

Detective Riggs uncrossed her arms. 'So, where's the footage? Your laptop? Office computer?'

Jason laughed. 'No. I'm not that tech savvy, to be honest. The guy who installed it set it up so the footage gets sent straight through to my office. It's on some kind of cloud somewhere, but I can access it from the office.'

'Okay, let's go there, then. I'll get one of my tech people to come with us.'

Jason shook his head. 'No need. I don't need a tech person, I have Rachel. Come on, let's go.'

———

At the office, Rachel was expecting them. As usual, she was dressed immaculately in a tailored suit with a silk scarf wrapped around her neck and her hair in a neat chignon. She ushered them both into the small conference room, where the computer was already set up on the table.

'I've taken the liberty of downloading the footage from the security system onto this computer,' Rachel said. 'I haven't seen it myself yet, but it's ready to go.' She looked at Jason. 'As you know, the cameras are triggered by a motion sensor, so you won't have to scroll through hours of nothing. Although sometimes they are set off by birds or people walking past the building.'

Jason sat down in one of the chairs at the conference room table, while Detective Riggs sat in the other. 'Thanks, Rach. Ready when you are.'

Rachel pressed the space bar and the screen filled with the feed from the different cameras positioned around the building site. 'As you can see, this shows all the cameras, but if you want to, we can look at the vision from any of the individual cameras as well.'

She pressed another button and a time stamp in one corner started counting forward from 10.45 pm. The camera that was positioned to show the front of the building had captured a group of people walking past. They moved off the screen, and then the time stamp flashed forward to 11.47 pm. One of the screens showed a bird in the dim security lighting. It pecked at something on the ground, caught an insect, and then flew off. The next time stamp showed an obviously drunk man walking past. He stopped to pee on the wall and then kept walking, staggering out of the frame. Jason was beginning to feel bored and frustrated. Then the time stamp jumped forward again – 2.56 am. At first, Jason couldn't see what had triggered the motion sensor. Probably just another bird, he thought, or worse still, a rat. But then he noticed a shadowy figure at the very edge of the screen, caught on the camera that showed the front of the site. He couldn't make out what the figure was doing.

'Hey Rach, can you enlarge that one?' he asked. She clicked a button and the feed filled the whole screen. The figure was still in the shadow, near the very edge of the camera's reach. Then Jason realised that the person was interfering with the security fence. Two of the panels of the tall mesh fencing separated and the figure disappeared into the gap. 'Woah, it should be impossible to separate those panels from the outside,' Jason said. 'Unless they weren't properly fitted.'

Detective Riggs shot him a glance. 'So that means someone on your crew has to be in on this. Someone left the pin out of those two security panels. That has to be someone on the inside.'

Jason shook his head. He was starting to get irritated. 'No. There's no way anyone on my crew has it in for me.'

Riggs looked at Rachel, eyebrows arched sceptically. 'Can you find the camera that shows the inside of this fence?'

Rachel nodded and navigated her way through the cameras until she found the one that showed the scaffolding at the front of the building. 'I'll take it back a little bit.'

When the footage played, Jason could see the two fence panels separate. Again, the figure on screen was at the furthest edge of the security camera's range. It was indistinct and shadowy, but he could tell it was a person of about medium height, probably a man, wearing all black, with a black cap on his head, and carrying a small backpack. The person moved to the scaffolding and began to climb. Very quickly they were out of range of the cameras, which showed only the first couple of levels of scaffolding. Maybe the vandal knew about the surveillance cameras, and that's why they chose to write their message so high up on the building. But how could they have known about the cameras? Even in daylight, if you didn't know the cameras were there it would be hard to spot them. At night time, it would be impossible. An inside job? As much as he hated to admit it, it was looking more likely. Jason felt a prickle of anger. Someone he trusted. Somehow, it made the situation much worse.

The cameras stayed on, probably triggered by the slight swaying of the scaffolding, as the vandal moved out of view. They knew what he was doing though – spraying his message across the front of the building and unbolting part of the scaffold. After a few minutes, the shadowy figure climbed down again. The man was obviously familiar with scaffolding. Or could it be a woman? He didn't think so, but it was possible.

'There was some damage inside as well, so maybe we'll get a better look at the bastard when he goes inside,' Jason said. The cameras were positioned to get good footage of anyone who went in or out of any of the building's entrances. Instead of going to one of the main entrances, the figure went to a small side door. Jason watched as the person on screen approached the doorway, cap pulled down to hide their face. There was something in the person's gait that seemed slightly familiar, but he couldn't think who it reminded him of. Then the person stood in front of the doorway and angled their body away from the camera, so the door handle was hidden from sight.

'Seems they definitely know about the cameras,' Riggs muttered. After a few seconds, the door opened and the person went inside. 'Do you think that door was left open?' she asked.

'No. No way,' Jason said. 'The ground floor doors are all lockable, and they're all checked every night by the foreman. There's a checklist and everything.'

Riggs took a deep breath but didn't say anything. Rachel toggled through the camera feeds until she found the one that showed the vandal. Again, the figure was only just visible at the far edge of the camera's field of vision. But it was obvious what they were doing. The figure was in a frenzy, smashing things with something in their hand, probably a heavy crowbar. After a few minutes, the frenzy stopped. And then the person carefully left the same way as they'd come in. Back out through the side door, cap pulled low to cover their face, and back through the gap in the security fencing. Then they disappeared into the darkness. And even though he hadn't been able to see the person's face, Jason couldn't shake the feeling there was something familiar about them. He knew that person, he was sure. He just couldn't think of who it might be.

CHAPTER 10

That afternoon, Jason sat in his car with his daughter. Inga had just finished her shift at the health-food shop, and when he arrived to give her a lift home, she appeared at the door with a smoothie in each hand. She had her usual sunshiny smile on her face, which lifted Jason's spirits, as always.

'It's smoothie weather, Dad. I got you one. You can have Mango Tango or Banana Blitz.'

Jason chose Mango Tango. 'Just what I needed!' They sat in the car in the parking lot, drinking the ice-cold smoothies, perfect for the Queensland weather, while Inga told him all about her day. Jason loved hearing about the little details of his kids' lives. Sometimes they seemed like mysterious strangers to him, and he wondered how they'd grown up so quickly. Then there were moments like this, drinking a Mango Tango while his daughter told him all about the difficult customers and the ones who'd made her laugh. In moments like this, he felt like all was right with the world.

'How about you, Dad?' Inga asked, between slurps of her Banana Blitz. 'What was your day like?'

Jason shrugged. 'A few hiccups at the building site, but nothing we can't handle.'

Inny frowned at him. Sometimes she had a sixth sense about when something was wrong. 'Come on Dad. What's going on? You never tell me stuff. I'm not a little kid, you know. I can handle it.'

That was true. He didn't like telling her anything negative or difficult. He didn't want to burden the kids with that kind of stuff. But his daughter was right. She was almost an adult, intelligent and independent, and she could handle hearing about the issues on the building site. Still, he tried to downplay the problems. 'We've just had some more damage to the site. Some more vandalism. Nothing major.' She listened as he told her about the damage to the scaffolding and the vandalism inside the building. He left out the part about the graffiti. He didn't want more questions about what that meant, and there was no way he wanted to explain that part of his past to his kid.

'That's really frustrating, Dad. You must be pissed off. Who do you think it is?'

He shrugged. 'No idea, really. Some kids with too much time on their hands. Someone with a grudge against me. Or maybe someone who has a financial interest in delaying our project.' He thought of Brian and his project that was so similar to his own. What would Brian do to get his apartments on the market first? It could be worth hundreds of thousands of dollars to him. Would he do something like this to get ahead in this game?

Inga smiled at him, slurping the last of her smoothie. 'So, what are you going to do about it, Dad?'

Jason returned her smile. 'First, I'm going to finish my smoothie. I'm going to enjoy every last drop. Then I'll drop you home. And then, I'm going to catch the bastard who's been doing this. Don't worry, Inga. I've got a plan.'

———

He did have a plan, although it was a fairly basic one. He'd admit that. So far, the vandalism had been happening once a week, and he thought the pattern would probably hold. He'd been thinking about what Detective Riggs had said about it possibly being an inside job. And maybe it was. He was completely confident in his crew but he couldn't dispute the evidence from the CCTV footage. Someone had deliberately set the security fence up so that the panels could be opened from the outside. And the vandal had easily been able to get inside the building. If it was an inside job, the ramped-up security and the video cameras weren't going to help. What he really needed was the element of surprise. It was a week since the last damage had taken place. They'd just gotten the mess cleaned up and the project back on schedule, more or less. And he had a gut feeling that the vandal would pay another visit tonight. This time, he'd be in for a surprise.

Before that, though, he had an important date planned. This time it wasn't with Mia. He was excited to see Mia again, and he'd phoned her earlier that day to ask her out for dinner. She'd said yes, enthusiastically.

'I must tell you, Jason, I haven't found out who the Galaxy owner is yet. They're hidden behind a wall of trusts and shell companies,' she'd told him.

'Well, I'm still interested in the Galaxy,' he'd said, 'but to be honest, I'm more interested in you.' Jason's policy with women had always been to be direct.

Mia had laughed a low, sexy laugh that sent a little tingle up his spine. 'You're a smooth talker. Well, dinner tomorrow night it is. I'll look forward to it.'

He was looking forward to dinner with Mia as well, but that would have to wait until tomorrow. He already had plans tonight that he couldn't break, with another woman who was very important to him. His Nan Dooksie. He went to pick up some takeaway and then headed in the direction of her cosy little house.

Nan met him at the door. She was short, with curly grey hair and a wicked sense of humour. Her blue eyes sparkled at him as she let him in. 'Still gunning to be my favourite grandson, are you Jason?' She glanced at the bag full of food. 'Good news for you, you're winning so far.'

Jason returned her grin. 'Ah Nan, I know it's not even a competition. Of course I'm your favourite. Don't worry, I won't tell the others.' He loved Nan Dooksie's cheeky sense of humour. In fact, he was pretty sure his own sense of humour was hereditary, passed down directly from her.

They took the food into the kitchen. Nan dished it up while she chatted, telling Jason all about her busy life. The area where she lived wasn't exactly a retirement village, but it might as well have been. It was full of little condos where many older people lived. Jason was always surprised at how many dramas went on between the retirees. Sometimes he felt as though his Nan was living on the set of *Days of Our Lives*. He'd said as much to her one day, and she'd winked at him. 'Oh, it's far more interesting around here than on *Days of Our Lives*, don't you worry.'

They chatted easily as they ate dinner. Nan had a bit of a sharp tongue – another thing that seemed to run in the family – but she loved spending time with her grandchildren and great grandchildren. Jason always felt at home in her company. His favourite time with her came after dinner. Nan pulled up a stool to her piano and began to play. She picked some songs that were old favourites for them both, and they both sang along as she played. Jason loved the fact he and his nan shared a love of music. He put aside all the thoughts about the building site, and everything else that was on his mind, and threw himself into the songs. There would be plenty of time to deal with vandals and building sites later on. For now, he was spending time with his nan, and that was all that mattered.

Later that evening, after saying goodnight to Nan, Jason turned his car back in the direction of Golden Sands. He didn't have much of a plan, but he had a gut feeling this was what he needed to do to in order to get to the bottom of the issues plaguing his construction site. And as someone who regularly relied on instinct, Jason knew it would not steer him wrong. There had been plenty of times in his life that his gut had saved him, or warned him, and a few times he hadn't listened and had ended up in hot water. In fact, the first time he'd seen the block of land where his development was currently going up, he knew it would be something special. And it still would be, he knew that. But first he had to deal with the asshole who was messing with his site.

As he got closer to the development, Jason drove past the Galaxy Nightclub. He checked the time on his car's display and realised it was nearly eleven o'clock. There was no line outside the Galaxy and very few people on the street. Not for the first time, he wondered what the deal was with that place. It clearly wasn't a profitable operation. Surely whoever owned it would be keen to sell? He liked Golden Sands, and he thought there was plenty of potential here. The Galaxy could become an amazing project. He remembered Rachel's frequent warnings about getting ahead of himself, but the ideas still swirled around in his head. That was fine; at this stage they were just ideas. He'd focus on that project when he'd sorted out this one. He wondered about the girl he'd seen there the night he and Pauly went to the Galaxy. What was her name? Stella? He hoped she was safe and that the guy who had been threatening her was staying well away.

He parked his car around the corner from the build site, just in case whoever was vandalising the site recognised it. From down the street he could hear the reverberating bass coming from the Galaxy. Further toward the beach the streets were crowded with people having a great time, but here, around the building site, it was quiet. A few people were sitting at tables at the restaurant over the road, but not many. It too was quiet. That didn't matter. When his development was finished, there would be much more life in this area. He could imagine a restaurant opening up on the ground floor, maybe a nice little wine bar or coffee shop too. It would be a wonderful place to live, but he had to get the damn project finished first.

He pulled the hood of his dark-coloured jumper over his head and walked toward the site. He unlocked the padlock hanging on the security fence, went in, and locked it behind him. At night, the only lighting on the site came from the streetlights. They threw long shadows over the building, changing its appearance. That suited him perfectly. He liked the shadows, and tonight he wanted to stay hidden. He walked through the site, noticing that everything seemed ordered and tidy, as he'd expect. There were tools stacked up against the walls here and there, nothing expensive, just shovels, wheelbarrows and a few things like that. The power tools would be locked away in the trailer at the back of the site or taken home by the tradies every night. Jason had thought about bringing some kind of weapon with him, but he'd decided against it. He didn't want to kill anyone, and he figured the vandal would be a coward. He just wanted to find out who it was, especially if it was someone on his crew.

He made his way through the half-lit yard to the side door the vandal had used last time. It was a good spot, he realised. The streetlights didn't illuminate much around this side of the building and the security camera was up quite high, so it wouldn't get a very good view of anyone coming in through this door. Jason found a spot nearby with a good view of the doorway and leaned up against the wall, making himself comfortable. He'd wait here til morning if he had to, but he hoped it wouldn't take that long.

It turned out he didn't have to wait very long at all.

CHAPTER 11

The figure came up the footpath from the direction of the Galaxy Nightclub. Jason spotted them as soon as they came close to the building site. In the shadowy half-light, it was only an outline in a dark hoodie and jeans. Even though he couldn't make out any features, Jason figured it was a man. It was the same person as on the security video, but in the flesh it was easier to make out the details. He was tall with a solid frame. The hood pulled down low over his forehead meant his face was shadowed.

Jason watched as the figure knelt close to the security fence. He heard the rasp of metal on metal. Maybe a pin being pulled from the fence? That shouldn't be possible from the outside, unless someone had deliberately set it up wrong. He made a mental note to check tomorrow. There was a scraping noise as the fence was pulled back just enough to open up a small gap between the panels. Jason stayed hidden in the shadows, keeping as still as he could. It wasn't natural for him – normally he was in perpetual motion – but he concentrated on slowing his breathing and keeping his eyes trained on the dark figure.

The man walked toward the side entrance of the building site, glancing around nervously. Again, there was something in his gait that seemed vaguely familiar. Jason just couldn't quite work out who it reminded him of. Still, he figured it didn't matter. In a minute or two he'd pull this bastard's hoodie back and find out exactly who it was. By now the man was close enough to Jason that he could spring up and grab him. But he stayed still. First, he wanted to see what the man was going to do.

He watched as the man slipped a key from his pocket and opened the side door. *Shit*. It really must be an insider if he had a key. He felt the slow burn of anger starting up in his gut. Someone on his crew, someone he trusted, was betraying him. Jason gave the other man a head start of a couple of seconds and then quietly slipped from his hiding spot. The intruder had left the door ajar, and Jason was grateful for new hinges on the door that didn't creak as he pushed the door open enough to enter.

The site was almost pitch-black inside, but ahead he could see a beam of light from the man's torch. He followed the pinprick of light through the site, until it stopped in the middle of the building's big foyer. Jason stopped, too, close enough that he could see what the man was doing, but not too close. The building was eerily quiet. In the torchlight, the man was a silhouette, although Jason could see he had something in his hand now. It looked like a heavy hammer. Unless the guy had really big pockets, it must have been hidden somewhere here at the site. Jason tensed, ready to spring before this asshole broke another thing. But instead, the guy held the hammer loosely in one hand, and took something out of his pocket. Then Jason could hear the unmistakable sound of a spray can being shaken.

For a moment he thought about letting the guy spray his weird cryptic message onto the wall. He wondered what it would be about this time. Some strange, half-remembered incident from his childhood? Something creepy that showed how obsessed this guy must be? More wondering and guessing if someone from his past had some kind of weird vendetta against him? A sudden burst of fury filled him. No. Enough of this bullshit. He wasn't going to wait around until the guy did his creative art project. He was going to put an end to things right now.

'Put down the spray can.' Jason stepped from the shadows. The intruder turned in his direction with a strangled yelp of surprise, the torchlight momentarily blinding him. In the thin beam of light, Jason could see that the man was still holding the hammer in one hand, fumbling to keep his grip on the torch and spray can in the other hand. The need for the torchlight won out and the man dropped the paint can, which rattled as it rolled to one side. Jason took a couple of steps forward. The stranger was not as tall as him, but was solidly built. He also had the advantage of a weapon. Jason only had his bare hands. But in an instant, all the carnage that this man had caused on his building site flashed through Jason's mind. He felt a surge of adrenaline. Was ready for a fight. He stepped forward again, clenching his fists to punch. The other man was obviously rattled, but darted forward and swung the hammer at Jason's head. Jason dodged it easily, once again thanking his brothers mentally for helping him develop quick reflexes. The room was dark, with the slender torch beam mostly serving to cast huge shadows on the bare walls.

He swung at the intruder, connecting with his jaw, but the hoodie, still pulled around the man's face, absorbed some of the impact. The stranger lunged wildly with the hammer, and Jason could hear his frantic breathing. His face was still in shadow. Once again, he dodged the hammer's blows by rocking back on his heels. The man was using the hammer claws first, and one of the claws glanced off Jason's arm as he swung wildly. Then Jason sprang forward while the other man was off balance and kicked at his knee. He could hear the sickening crunch as he connected, and the other man yelped in pain. He prepared for another wild lunge with the hammer, expecting to have to dodge and duck. What he wasn't expecting was for the other man to run. Jason lunged forward, trying to catch the intruder. Instead of fighting back, the man let out a strangled yelp. He darted around Jason and ran for the doorway. Jason turned and sprinted after him, but the man was a fraction faster. The loss of the torch beam didn't help. Jason stumbled on some steps, cursing his stiff back, and just missed catching the other man as he pushed through the still-open side door.

Instead of running toward the front of the site where the gap in the security fencing was, the other man ran toward the back of the building. Jason followed, cursing his lack of fitness as he ran. The other man was limping and breathing hard. He made up for his lack of speed by doing all he could to slow Jason down. This was obviously someone who knew the site well. Jason managed to dodge the random items the other man pulled into his path. Shovels, lengths of pipe, even wheelbarrows were thrown back at him by the escaping vandal. He dodged the barrage of tools and narrowly avoided stepping on a piece of piping. The glow from the streetlights down the street was dim, but still he managed to avoid the trolley that the other man flung back at him. But all the ducking and dodging slowed him down enough that the other man was able to climb up on a pallet of bricks that stood by the back security fence. Then he swung his legs over the fence and dropped down to the other side, cursing as he landed on the injured knee. Jason could hear his uneven footsteps as he ran down the alley. *Step, drag, step, drag.*

By now, Jason was panting hard. He felt too wary about his back to attempt a flying leap over the fence, even with the benefit of the pallet of bricks. So instead, he watched as the faint torch beam disappeared down the alley. Damn, he wasn't as fast as he used to be. He'd almost had the guy. He cursed his lack of foresight – of course he should have realised the guy would run. He should have been prepared for that, not just prepared for a fight. He should have brought a damn torch, at least. As the adrenaline faded, a nagging thought remained. There was a familiar feel about the intruder. It was someone he knew, he felt sure. He just didn't know who it was.

———

The next morning Jason stood at the front of the construction site waiting for Detective Riggs to arrive. He was holding a cup of coffee, which he felt he needed after the late night, and an extra one for Riggs. She arrived in an unmarked squad car, squealing the tyres as she slid to a stop in front of the site.

'Morning, Detective.' Jason greeted her as she got out of the car. He held out the coffee for her. 'I don't know how you take your coffee, but this is a flat white with one sugar. I reckon that will do the trick.'

Riggs looked taken aback, but took the cup. 'Thanks,' she said stiffly. 'I need a coffee.' She took a sip. 'Lucky guess, too. This is just how I take it.' She gave him the tiniest hint of a smile, then it was back to business. 'So, do you want to fill me in? You said on the phone you were at the site last night.'

Jason drank some of his own drink. So far, he was pleasantly surprised with the quality of the coffee in Golden Sands. 'Yep. I had a feeling the vandal would be back, so I decided to wait around and see if I could catch them in the act.'

Riggs frowned at him. 'You're not a police officer, you know. That was a dangerous thing to do.'

Jason shrugged. 'Dangerous to hang out at my own building site? Of course not. I should be able to come and go whenever I want. Anyway, don't you want to know if anyone turned up?'

She glared at him. 'Okay. Did anyone break into the site?'

'Yes, as a matter of fact, they did, detective. I caught them in the act.' He took a sip of coffee.

'You what? You caught someone here? Who was it?'

'Well, sadly I didn't manage to find that out.' Jason described the events of the evening to the detective. 'Unfortunately, I'm not quite as fast as I used to be. The guy got away.' He pulled the spray can from his pocket, carefully wrapped in a ziplock bag. 'I did get you a present, though, detective. The guy dropped this. He wasn't wearing gloves. Well, at least not as far as I could see. So, it should have prints on it.'

Riggs took the ziplock bag, still glaring at him. 'You realise that even if we do get some usable prints off this can, I've only got your word that it was found at the site. And you're a suspect in this case as well, Jason. For all I know you're doing this for the insurance money.'

Jason laughed. 'Well, that just shows you don't know anything about me at all, detective. I'd rather run naked through a thorn bush than have to deal with insurance companies. Plus, why would I need to? The most important thing to me at this stage is getting the build finished on time. Anything else is going to cost me money.'

She frowned. 'You realise I can't just take your word for it.'

Jason shook his head. Damn, he should have got them to put an extra couple of sugars in the detective's coffee. She needed sweetening up this morning. 'You're forgetting about the cameras. That should confirm my story.'

She paused, then nodded. 'Right. We'd better go and take a look at them, then.'

Jason shook his head. 'I don't need to look at the cameras. I was there, remember? If you go to the office, Rachel will be able to show you everything. I need to make sure everything is on track here on site.'

Riggs frowned but didn't argue. Jason figured that by now she'd worked out there wasn't any point in arguing with him. He was stubborn enough to out-argue anyone. Except his kids. They'd got their stubbornness from him. 'Right,' she said. 'I'll go and check out the footage, and then I'll take this to the lab. Let's hope there are some usable prints.'

Jason hoped the footage from the security cameras might be clear enough to show the intruder's face, but either way, he felt certain the bastard would think twice before coming back to the site. He remembered the crunch the man's knee had made when he'd given it the side kick last night. At the very least, he thought, the man would be walking with a limp for a little while. He hoped that one way or another, that would be the last of the vandalism and they could get the project back on schedule.

'Thanks for the coffee,' Riggs said as she got back into her car. Jason smiled and lifted his own cup in a salute. He turned back to the building site. There were a few workers in high-vis milling around on the front footpath, and he could see a few more sitting on a pallet of bricks by the front of the building. He grimaced. Frank should have them all moving by now.

'Boss,' one of the chippies called. Jason glanced over. It was a young guy called Phil who'd been on the crew for a while now. He was a good, reliable worker, one of the regulars.

'Hey, Phil,' Jason greeted the man. 'Where's Frank? He needs to get these apprentices to work.' He gestured to the young guys sitting on the pallet of bricks.

'That was what I was going to ask you,' Phil said. 'He's not here yet. I've got a key, so I let the fellas in this morning. Sometimes Frank's a little late, you know, if there's traffic and stuff. But he should be here by now.'

Jason checked his phone. It was nearly nine o'clock. For a building site, it was nearly smoko already. There were a few notifications on his screen, but no calls or texts from Frank. Strange. He was a cranky old bastard at the best of times, but he was reliable. It wasn't like him not to show up for work. 'Can you get the guys started, Phil? I'll give Frank a call and see what's going on.'

'Yeah, no worries, Jason, but I've already tried calling him. It just rings out. Maybe he'll answer for you.' Phil went off toward the site, shouting at the apprentices sprawled out on the bricks on his way past. The two young guys sprang up and scurried after him.

Jason found Frank's name and pressed the button to dial. He held the phone to his ear. It rang until it eventually went to voicemail. Jason didn't bother leaving a message. Instead, he scrolled through his phone until he found Frank's wife's phone number. Sandra, that was her name. He dialled and, after a moment, a cheery voice answered.

'Sandra, how are you? It's Jason. Sorry to be phoning you.'

'No trouble at all, Jason. What can I do to help?'

'Look, I don't want to worry you, Sandra, but Frank hasn't turned up at the site this morning. And I can't reach him on his phone.' Jason had a sudden vision of Frank being in a car accident somewhere, his phone ringing fruitlessly as he lay trapped under crushed metal.

'Oh, didn't he tell you?' Sandra didn't sound worried at all. 'He had to go to the doctor this morning. He was in a bit of a fluster, he must have forgotten to call you.'

Jason felt a sense of foreboding starting in the pit of his stomach. This was worse than the car accident idea. 'Is he okay, Sandra?'

'Oh yes, he's fine. Silly bugger. Just tripped on some stairs last night. Must have been a bit drunk, I think. He'd been out late at the pub.'

'Tripped on some stairs? What's he done to himself?' Jason knew what she was going to say before the words even came out of her mouth.

'Oh, it's his knee. He's really done a number on it.'

'I see. Thanks Sandra.' Jason hung up the phone as he felt the sense of things clicking into place. The feeling of familiarity when he saw the vandal on the video cameras, and then at the site last night. Now he knew who it reminded him of. Someone he knew really well, with a distinctive, rolling gait. His foreman. Frank.

He lifted his phone again and dialled Detective Riggs's number.

'Detective, I think I know who's vandalised the site. We have a suspect.' But even as he said the words, he felt a sense of unease. Something didn't feel right about that at all.

CHAPTER 12

Jason and Frank had been friends for a long time. In fact, they'd known each other since they were kids. Back then, Frank had been lanky and laid-back, with scruffy hair and a habit of daydreaming in class. They'd knocked around the same neighbourhood together, riding bikes and hanging out in each other's houses until someone's mum got sick of them and sent them outside. Then they'd go to the next house to eat snacks and cause trouble. On hot days, if they were lucky, they'd swim in Richie's pool, and if not, they'd set up a sprinkler on someone's front lawn and run through it until they were dripping wet and sunburnt.

He and Frank had lost touch a bit during their teenage years as Frank had gone to a different high school, but they still ran into each other from time to time. Then they'd worked together back in Jason's early deck-building days. Back then, Frank had lived for surfing, and work was merely the way he could afford food and fuel. But then he'd married, had a couple of kids and settled down a bit. Well, as far as Jason knew, anyway. He obviously didn't know Frank as well as he thought he did. He would never in a million years have guessed it was Frank who was vandalising his project.

But still, friendship had to mean something, right? It meant something to Jason, even if it obviously didn't mean much to Frank. And, as a friend, he couldn't just send the cops around to Frank's place to arrest him. He had to at least give his mate the benefit of the doubt and talk to him first. So he'd told Detective Riggs he'd meet her at the police station in a couple of hours, then got into his car. Frank's place wasn't too far away. He spent the fifteen-minute drive listening to Cold Chisel and belting out all the lyrics. It was a good distraction.

When he knocked on Frank's front door, Sandra opened it. She was a small blonde woman with a worried look on her face. 'Oh. Jason.' She seemed surprised to see him. 'Frank's still not home. I guess he must have been held up at the doctor. Is everything okay?'

He smiled, trying to reassure the woman. 'Yeah, of course, Sandra. I just need to talk to Frank about something fairly urgent, so I thought I'd come past in person. Can you tell me the address of his doctor? I'll go past and see if I can catch him there.'

The worry didn't leave the woman's face, but she nodded and found the doctor's address for him. Jason wanted to say something reassuring, but her husband might be in a whole heap of shit, so he thought it might be better to say nothing. He thanked her and headed back to the car. The doctor's office was just around the corner, and even though Jason couldn't see Frank's ute in the car park, he stopped anyway and went inside. Frank wasn't in the waiting room either.

'Hello, can I help you?' asked the receptionist, a cheery young man.

'Yes, I'm just looking for my friend Frank. I need to talk to him urgently. He must be in with the doctor at the moment, so I'll wait.'

'Oh.' The young man looked surprised. 'Look, I'm not sure if I'm supposed to tell you, but I guess if it's urgent. There's no-one here by the name of Frank at the moment.' He checked the monitor in front of him. 'Hmm. No, he's definitely not here.'

Jason thanked him and headed back out. Of course not. What had he expected? But still, he knew what Frank's car looked like, and he didn't have anything else he needed to do that morning. He drove a few loops around the neighbourhood, checking out different areas where he thought Frank might be. Sure enough, a couple of blocks away he saw the battered ute parked near a pretentious-looking pub called The Grantham

Arms. Jason went inside, suppressing the urge to roll his eyes at the timber panelled walls and oversized paintings of English hunting scenes hanging on them. The pub was almost empty, but down the end of the long timber bar, with a half-empty pint glass of beer in front of him, was Frank. Jason walked down to where he was sitting and said, 'Hi Frank.'

Frank almost fell off his seat. Alarmed, he pushed himself off and stood next to the bar stool. Jason could see he wasn't putting much weight on his left leg. 'Something the matter with your knee, mate?'

Frank's face was pale and he gripped the edge of the bar. He looked around, scanning anxiously for an exit, but gave up. To get to the exit he'd have to get past Jason. He obviously did the maths and decided that with his knee in that condition, the odds weren't in his favour. He gave a heavy sigh and sat back down on the stool. 'Yeah. Knee's fucked.'

Jason nodded, sitting down on the stool next to Frank. He gestured to the barman and gestured to the beer in front of Frank. The barman poured him a pint of a liquid the same shade. Jason pulled a bill out of his wallet and handed it over without looking at him. 'Get up to much last night, mate?' he asked. Frank shook his head, looking determinedly down into his drink, and Jason decided to cut to the chase. 'Come on, Frank. I know it was you there last night. What the absolute fuck? I thought you were my friend.'

Frank sighed again. 'Yeah. Well, what can I say?'

'You can start by explaining to me why you were vandalising the building site.'

Frank took a swig of beer. 'I shouldn't be saying anything without a lawyer.'

Jason lifted his eyebrows. 'Right. Well, if you'd prefer to explain things to Detective Riggs, I'm sure that can be arranged. But after all our years of knowing each other, I thought you'd be man enough to tell me to my face why the fuck you've been messing with my site.'

Frank swung around on his seat to face Jason, a hard expression crossing his face. 'Money troubles, okay? I've been having a few money issues, and some bastard offered me money to spray-paint some weird messages on the walls and smash some of the pipes and wiring. So I took it. I figured you'd be fine. You've got insurance, haven't you?'

Jason could feel his muscles tensing with anger. The bored-looking barman wandered over but Jason waved him away and turned back to Frank. 'Money troubles? Aren't I paying you enough? Why didn't you come to me, ask for a raise, mate? You know I would have given it to you. What the hell do you need money for, anyway?'

Frank shook his head sadly. 'That wouldn't do it, Jason.' He paused for a while, obviously deciding how much to say. 'I've got this gambling debt. I mean, it's just gotten out of control. I told Sandra I'd stop with the cards, but by then I already owed a lot. I thought I'd have one more go, just to win enough to wipe some of the debt.' He shrugged. 'I'm sure you can guess how that went. I just managed to dig the hole even deeper. It was the only way I could get out of it.'

'Come on man, why didn't you just come to me? You know I would have helped you out.'

Something hard and bitter passed across Frank's face. 'Yeah sure. You know how humiliating that would have been? Coming to you with my fuck-ups and expecting a handout?'

Jason's frustration was rising. 'So you think the solution was to mess with the building site? You're fucking kidding me, right?'

Frank turned to him, anger flashing in his eyes. 'You don't know these guys I owe money to, Jason. They're real mean. I'm scared they might do something to hurt Sandra or the kids. Look, I don't expect you to understand, but I had to do it.'

'Okay, well why those messages? What did they mean?'

Frank shrugged. 'No clue, mate. I just wrote what I was told to write.'

'By the person who was paying you to vandalise the site?'

'Yeah.'

'So, who was that? I figure the least you can do is tell me who has enough of a vendetta against me that they'll pay someone to vandalise my site.'

Jason could see Frank shut down. His demeanour felt bitter and angry, but underneath it, Jason could sense fear. Frank was afraid of something. Or someone. 'Honestly, mate. I don't know who it was. I just got a phone call, then money appeared in my mailbox in a brown paper bag. No idea who it was.' Then, without another word, he drained the rest of his beer, stood up and limped to the door.

———

Jason's phone rang as he was leaving the pub. He glanced at the screen and realised it was Mia. He answered. 'Hey, beautiful. What's going on?'

'Hi Jason.' He could hear the warmth in her voice. 'How did you go last night?'

He laughed. 'It was eventful, to say the least.' He gave her a run-down of the events of the previous night, and then told her about confronting Frank at the pub. 'He's the vandal, that's for sure. But there's someone else who's behind this, Mia. Someone was paying him to graffiti my site. He won't tell me who it was, but I'll get it out of him.'

Mia sounded thoughtful. 'Right. You've got to wonder what that person's motivation is, don't you? And why the cryptic messages?'

'That's what I'm planning to figure out.'

'In the meantime, Jason, I've found out a bit more about the Galaxy. Some interesting things are going on in that place.' Jason's phone buzzed as she was speaking, and he glanced at the screen. Another call was coming in. It was Inga. He usually wouldn't interrupt a beautiful woman like Mia, but this was his daughter.

'Hey Mia, I've got another call coming in. It's my daughter, so I'd better take it. Can I call you back?'

'Oh, no problem. Are we still on for dinner? I can just tell you tonight.'

'Of course. I've made the reservation already, and am looking forward to it.'

'Great. I'll see you then.' She hung up and Jason tried to switch over to the incoming call from his daughter. As usual, his tech skills failed him and he managed to hang up on her by accident, but he rang her right back.

'Inny! Sorry, I was trying to answer the call and I accidentally sent it to voicemail.'

She laughed. 'All good, Dad. I know what you're like.'

'What's up, Inny? You off to work today?'

'No, I'm actually on my way now. I'm on the bus. I just thought I'd give you a call.'

'You should have called me! I could have picked you up and taken you there!' He had friends who grumbled and complained about being their kids' taxi services, but Jason was always happy to drive his kids around to work and sport and all the other things they packed into their busy schedules. Some of the best conversations he'd had with them were spontaneous chats in the car on the way to work or school.

'Nah, it's all good, Dad. I know you're busy, and I don't want to make you drive me all over the city. Plus, I don't mind the bus.'

'Well, if you're sure. I really don't mind driving you places, you know.' By now, he'd walked back to his car. He opened the door and sat in the driver's seat, leaving the door open to let some fresh air into the car.

'I know, Dad. But that's not why I rang.' She paused for a moment, gathering her thoughts before she continued. 'I was going to tell you something, but you've got to promise me you won't freak out, okay? It's really not a big deal.'

'Heyyy,' he put on a fake offended tone. 'I don't freak out about anything. Don't know what you're talking about, kiddo.'

She laughed. 'Come on, Dad. You have to promise. Don't get all overprotective on me, will you?'

'Right. I promise. I'll be as calm as a cucumber. Now, tell me what's up.' He wasn't sure what to expect, but Inga was a responsible, sensible kid, wise beyond her years. He was sure it wouldn't be anything to worry about.

'So, I've noticed this thing over the last few days, and like I said, it's really no big deal. It's just a bit weird. I think someone has been following me.'

In an instant, Jason was on high alert. 'Following you? What do you mean?'

'Well, like, on Tuesday when I walked to work from my friend's place, someone was walking behind me the whole way. I couldn't see them that well, but it looked like a young guy wearing a black hoodie and jeans. Then when I went home after my shift, I saw the same kid in the car park, just hanging around. And yesterday I saw them again, when I was on the bus heading home.'

It was taking every inch of Jason's self-control to keep his voice calm. 'Is this guy on the bus with you now?' The attacks on his work site were one thing, and he didn't care who came after him. He'd handle it. But if anyone so much as harmed a single hair on his kids' heads, he would track them down and tear off their limbs with his bare hands.

'Nah. But I think I saw him near the bus stop when I was getting on the bus. That's why I rang you.'

'Inny, I'm coming right away. I'll meet you at your work.'

'Dad, seriously. It's not a big deal.'

'I know, Inga, but if anything ever happened to you, I'd…' he trailed off. He didn't know what he'd do, because the idea of anything happening to his daughter was something he never wanted to even think about. It was his worst nightmare. He kept his voice calm. 'I'm not going to make a big deal of it. But I am going to come in and chat to you in person about this. And make sure you're safe. Look, there are some things going on at my work site, and I just want to make sure there's no connection with that.' He had an itching feeling that the guy who was following Inga was connected with the vandalism on the site. In fact, his gut was telling him he did for sure.

Inny sighed in resignation. 'Okay Dad. I'll see you soon.'

Jason sat in the car, his pulse galloping. He trusted Inga. She was a sensible kid – well, pretty much an adult now. But he had to make sure she was safe. He would keep his promise to stay cool as a cucumber, but he was damn sure going to protect his daughter.

CHAPTER 13

etective Riggs might have been a pain in the arse generally, but when Jason told her about the guy who was following his daughter, she came right away. It took a bit of convincing because Inga didn't want the fuss, but eventually she agreed to have a police officer escort her home after her shift. She also promised she wouldn't go out alone until the issues with the build site had been resolved. Jason enfolded her into a huge hug. 'I'm sorry, Inga. I know it's annoying, but it's just until we sort out these issues. Then I promise I'll stop being overprotective.'

Inga laughed and rolled her eyes at him. 'Sure Dad, like that's going to happen. Now I really have to go. I'm so late already.' She flounced off to start her shift, leaving him in the parking lot with Riggs.

'I wouldn't worry about it, Jason,' Riggs tried to reassure him. 'I'm sure it's just kids playing a prank, or maybe a lovesick admirer. Something like that. Plus, it looks like we've found your vandal anyway. We've got your man Frank down at the station for questioning, and it's not looking good for him.'

Jason kept his tone light. 'I'm sure you're right, detective, but I'm not taking any chances when it comes to my kids.'

He couldn't shake the feeling of unease. It might have been Frank who was vandalising the site, but someone else was behind the whole mess. He was sure of it. And whoever it was had a vendetta against him for some reason.

'We'll keep an eye on your daughter, Jason.' Riggs cracked the smallest of smiles. 'I know what it's like. I've got teenagers as well, and they hate anything that interferes with their independence. We'll keep an eye on her from a distance.'

Jason glanced at the steely detective. Maybe she was human after all. 'Thanks, Detective Riggs. I appreciate it.'

The detective said goodbye and got into her car. Jason's thoughts turned toward Jaxson. If the creep with the vendetta was following Inga around, maybe he was doing the same with Jax. The thought made Jason's blood boil. He pulled his phone out of his pocket and dialled while he was walking back toward the car. Jax answered right away. 'Hey Dad. What's up?'

'Jax!' Jason felt his heart swell with joy just at the sound of his son's voice. 'Where are you?'

'I'm at the tennis courts, Dad. Just finished a coaching session, and I've got another one coming up soon.'

'Right. Stay put, I'll be there in ten minutes.' Jason rang off and gunned the car in the direction of the tennis club.

———

Jason found his son standing under a shelter shading one of the tennis courts, watching a game between two boys who looked in their early teens. One of the boys, a skinny kid with a shock of blond hair, was winning easily, hitting shots with confidence and making his opponent run wildly around the court.

Jax smiled a greeting as Jason approached, gesturing toward the blond boy. 'I've been coaching this kid for a few months now. He's making pretty good progress, isn't he?' They watched for a couple of minutes as Jax's protégé wiped the floor with the other kid.

Jason's heart swelled with pride. Jax was tall and handsome, with his mum's blonde hair and slim build, but his determination, drive and restless energy surely came directly from his father. 'He's a good player. You've done a great job, Jax.'

'Thanks, Dad.' Jaxson looked over at him quizzically. 'Is everything okay?'

'Yeah, of course. I just wanted to ask you if you've noticed anything strange going on around here. Anyone following you, or threatening you?'

Jax frowned in concentration. 'Nah, I don't think so. Why's that?'

Jason gave his son a quick run-down of the events on the building site, and his phone call with Inga that morning. 'Some weirdo is out to get me, and I guess they've decided the best way to get to me is through my kids. I'll be damned if I'm going to let that happen.'

Jax looked off into the distance. 'Now you mention it, Dad. It could just be a coincidence, but there's been a strange guy hanging around the tennis club a bit in the last few days. Big guy, dressed all in black. Obviously not here to play tennis, cause he's wearing jeans and boots. And dark sunglasses. I've been keeping an eye on him because he gives me the creeps a bit. I thought he might have been stalking one of the girls or something.'

Jason felt a flash of fire run through his veins. He was going to find whoever was behind all this and tear them limb from limb. No more Mr Nice Guy. This was serious now.

He kept his tone calm despite the tension running through his body. 'Have you seen him around today, Jax?'

'No, not that I can think of.' Jax lifted his head and looked around him, scanning the club's perimeter like an army scout. Jason followed the boy's gaze. Everything seemed perfectly normal. Just the usual preppy kids wearing tennis outfits and sporty men and women in a variety of activewear, all looking like they belonged. There were a few spectators around the courts on this side of the clubhouse, but again, no-one who looked out of place, and certainly no-one dressed all in black with dark glasses.

Jason turned back to his son. 'Jax, do me a favour, okay? If you see this guy again, give me a call right away. And be careful, won't you, son? Whoever's behind this is unpredictable and probably dangerous.' He thought of the fear that flashed across Frank's face. There was real fright behind that look. And he was damn sure going to keep his kids away from it.

Jax nodded. 'Sure, Dad. I'll be careful. I'm sure it's nothing, though. Maybe just someone who wanted to join the club or something.' He glanced at his watch. 'I need to head to my next coaching session. It's on the other side of the clubhouse.'

'I'll walk with you,' Jason said. He enjoyed seeing his son at the tennis club, where he seemed to be in his natural habitat. It suited him.

Jax picked up his tennis racquet and backpack from one of the chairs and the two of them walked toward the clubhouse. They followed a path through the neatly manicured grounds to the courts on the far side of the club. Jax had booked one of the courts furthest from the building, close to the parking lot. A row of tall pines along one side of the grounds shielded the houses beyond from any stray tennis balls. Jason had always admired the stately row of trees. He was gazing at them when he spotted the man, standing in the shadow of the tree on the end of the row. Jax must have spotted him at the same time. 'Oh! That's him.'

Adrenaline was coursing through Jason's veins, and he broke into a run. When he was younger, he'd been fast. And he still had it, mostly, despite his bad back. For a moment, he didn't think about it. He felt his feet pounding the pavement, his long strides eating up the distance between him and the man under the tree. He was going to pay for this tomorrow, but for now, he didn't care. He was going to catch that bastard if it was the last thing he did.

It took a few seconds for the man under the tree to realise that Jason was running in his direction, then another moment for him to decide what to do. He chose to run, but unfortunately for him, the row of trees where he was standing was inside the tall fence surrounding the club. He darted toward the gate out into the parking lot, scrambling as quickly as a man his size and build could. Jason wasn't going to let him get away that easily. He could hear his own pulse hammering in his ears, leaning forward and running like hell as the fire in his veins propelled him onward. For a split second, he felt as though he was back in Woodridge, thundering down the footpath with his brothers close behind him. He felt the same weightless energy moving him headlong through the gate and out into the parking lot, sprinting behind the man in black.

Jason reached the stranger in black halfway through the parking lot and grabbed his arm, using his momentum to help him spin the man around. He wanted to see this guy's face before he decked him. 'What the fuck are you doing here? Why are you following my son?' he shouted. The other man's eyes were open wide in fear or shock, and in that moment, Jason felt a flash of recognition. He'd seen this guy before, in the Galaxy Nightclub the night he'd been out with Pauly. He'd been one of the bouncers, the one who'd asked him to leave after he'd intervened to help the girl – Stella? That was her name, right?

'Let go of my fucking arm,' the man growled. He was obviously not planning on talking. But Jason didn't feel like talking anyway. He wanted to send a message. He swung his fist at the other man's face, putting all his weight behind the right hook. It connected, and he could feel the impact of his knuckles on the guy's cheekbone. Jason stepped forward, grabbing the front of the guy's jacket as he staggered back. He was big and broad-shouldered. But there was something about Jason's fierce energy that had knocked him off balance.

'Leave my kids alone. Tell your boss to stop being a fucking coward and face me one on one,' he shouted.

It took a moment for the man in black to recover from the punch, but when he did, he stepped forward, fists swinging wildly in Jason's direction. The guy was at least as tall as him and built like a brick shithouse, but that didn't make him a good shot. Jason dodged most of the punches, but one blow glanced across his mouth. He tasted blood and felt another jolt of adrenaline. Then he swung his weight forward and his fist connected with the other side of the guy's face.

There was the unmistakable crunch of a broken nose, and the man in black staggered backward. Jason was determined to knock the bastard out so he could call Riggs and get her to haul him off to her interrogation room and get some answers out of him. He landed another punch on the man's jaw as he fumbled for something in the pocket of his jacket. Jason saw the glint of light on metal, and then it was his turn to jump backward, dodging the flick-knife that was swinging in his direction.

The man's eyes were wild and there was blood streaming from his nose. Jason dodged the blade. Then, taking advantage of Jason's step backward, the man turned and ran. He was fast. He made it to a nondescript white Corolla, threw open the door and piled inside. Jason was right behind him. He thought about grabbing the door and hauling the man out, but what would that achieve? He'd made his point fairly clearly.

The white Corolla peeled out of the parking lot, tyres squealing on the bitumen. As his fear dissipated, Jason realised he hadn't got the numberplate. He kicked himself mentally, then turned and saw his son standing nearby.

Jax let out a low whistle. 'You got in a couple of good punches there, Dad. Not bad, old man,' he joked.

Jason shook his fist. 'Well, hopefully he won't be back. I only wish I'd got the guy's numberplate, so we could give it to the cops. And to the tennis club's security.'

Jax smiled and held up his phone. 'I got it, Dad. And a couple of good photos of the guy. In fact, I think I got an action shot of your fist connecting with his face, too.'

Jason laughed and slung his arm around his son's shoulders. 'Awesome! Great work, Jax. That'll really help.' He touched a finger to his split lip and winced. 'Damn, the bastard got me.'

Jax smiled. 'It doesn't look too bad, Dad. As long as you're not planning on kissing anyone tonight, you should be fine.'

———

Jason was planning on kissing someone that night. But first things first. He had to make sure his kids were safe, so he checked in with them both. Inga was planning to stay home with her mother that night, and Jason reminded her to check that the security system was turned on. Jax was at a friend's house, and he promised he wouldn't go out on his own. With the tension of the day dissipating, he finally felt like he could relax. His kids were safe – for now, anyway.

He picked up Mia from her house, which turned out to be a stark white condo in a fashionable part of town. She came to the door wearing a figure-hugging black dress that accentuated her curves and made his pulse jump. 'My god, Mia, you look amazing,' he said, taking her hand.

She smiled at him, her dark eyes looking him over. 'You look quite fine yourself.' She stepped in closer to him, and he could smell the sweet scent of her perfume. 'What's happened to your lip?' She ran her finger gently over the split lip, sending a tingle of desire through Jason.

He shrugged. 'It's nothing. Just got into a little tangle with one of the goons from the Galaxy earlier today. He was following one of my kids.' He laughed. 'I got off pretty lightly compared to him.'

Mia's eyes widened. 'Oh no, Jason, that's terrible. Are your kids okay?'

'Yeah, they're fine. Takes more than a stupid goon following them around to scare them. They're tough.' Mia was looking up at him with wide eyes, close enough that he could easily lean forward and kiss her. But not yet. The night was only beginning. Instead, he took her hand and brought it to his lips. Her skin was soft and warm. 'Come on, we'd better get to the restaurant. Otherwise, we might not make it out of the house.'

She smiled mischievously. 'Would that be a bad thing?' But she reached for her purse and followed him out of the front door. 'I'll tell you all about what I found out about the Galaxy on the way to the restaurant.'

CHAPTER 14

Jason woke to the buzzing of his mobile phone. For a moment, he couldn't place exactly where he was. Then the very pleasant memories of the previous night came flooding back. The dinner had been wonderful, and everything that came afterwards… well, that had been wonderful too. Mia was still asleep beside him, breathing rhythmically. His phone was still buzzing. Jason fumbled around beside the bed and found it. He glanced at the screen. It was 2 am and the incoming call was from Sandra, Frank's wife. Jason didn't answer. Why the hell was Sandra calling at this hour of the night? His brain went into overdrive, thinking of all the possible scenarios.

The most likely one was that Frank was in some kind of trouble. Jason rolled his eyes. Frank was big enough to deal with his own problems. The police had taken him in for questioning yesterday and charged him with malicious damage, but they'd let him go late in the afternoon on bail. The build site had been closed down so the forensic team could go over it, but Riggs had promised him they'd only need a day. So, the crew had today off. But either way, Frank wasn't going to be coming back to work. That ship had sailed for good. Jason glanced at Mia, who was starting to stir on the other side of the bed, and threw his phone back on the side table. He'd call Sandra back later.

The phone rang again. Cursing softly, he picked it up. Sandra again. He sighed with resignation and answered it. As he did, he swung out of bed, slipping quietly away so he didn't wake Mia.

'Jason? I'm sorry to ring you in the middle of the night.'

'It's fine, Sandra. What's up?' He tried to keep his voice low.

'It's Frank. I'm just… I'm worried, Jason. He got a phone call about fifteen minutes ago. Then he left the house. Said he had to check on the build site. I thought that was a bit strange at this time of night, but you know Frank. He can be a bit secretive sometimes, and there's no use questioning him.'

Yeah, he is, gambling his family's money away without anyone knowing, Jason thought. He felt a jolt of anger. Frank had everything going for him and he was pissing it all away by gambling and getting involved with the wrong kind of people. He felt sorry for Sandra. 'And?' he prompted her to continue.

'Well, it's just that about ten minutes ago I got a strange text from him. I couldn't sleep after he went out, so I was just lying here, awake. The text said, "No matter what happens, remember I love you." And now he's not answering his mobile.' She dissolved into tears.

Shit. 'And you have no idea where he might be?'

'Well, no. He just said the building site…' she trailed off. 'I guess he's not supposed to be there now, is he?' Sandra had found out about the charges against Frank when she came to bail him out. She'd been upset, but not really surprised.

'No, he's not.' The building site. Jason's blood ran cold. He had a bad feeling about this.

'Okay.' Sandra's voice sounded soft. She was worried, and for good reason. Jason felt sure it wasn't going to be good news.

'Listen, Sandra, I'll go and see if I can find him. Maybe ask some of the fellas. In the meantime, just sit tight. And can you call me right away if he turns up?'

'Sure.' Sandra sounded relieved he was taking charge of the situation. 'Thanks Jason.'

He rang off. Mia was awake now, gazing up at him in a way that put a streak of fire in him. Oh god, he was going to kill Frank for this.

The last thing he wanted to do was leave this bed. 'Hey, beautiful.' He bent to kiss her. 'I'm so sorry, did I wake you?'

She stretched and rolled over toward him. 'Hmm, that's okay. I don't mind waking up for a hot guy.' Her voice was low and sexy. 'Is everything okay?'

He groaned with frustration. 'I can't believe this, but I have to go.' He told Mia about the phone call from Sandra. 'Believe me, it's the last thing I want to do, but I need to go check the site. It's locked up at this time of night and there are security cameras. But I just have this feeling... I've got a young bloke, Timmons, coming to open up for the forensic team and receive a few deliveries of materials we're expecting this morning. I just... well, if something's gone on there, I don't want Timmons to be first on the scene. He doesn't need that.' The kid was hardworking and reliable, but he was young. Jason didn't know what to expect, but he figured he'd better get there first.

'That's fine,' Mia said, running a finger down his arm. 'Go and do what you have to. We can always pick this up later on.' She gave him a hot, smouldering look.

Jason kissed her again, long and slow. He knew he had a tiny fraction of willpower left to get out of this room before he forgot about Frank and Timmons and the rest of the whole damn world and stayed here with Mia forever. It was only the tiniest fragment, but it was enough. He pulled on his clothes and left.

On the way to the site he thought about what Mia had told him the evening before. She'd talked to a few of her clients who had connections in the area, and they'd all told her the same thing. The Galaxy was notorious for being the centre of a drug distribution ring. Apparently, it was an open secret. Jason was new to the area, so of course they were going to clam up when he asked about the old nightclub. But Mia was a familiar face, someone who'd been living and working in Golden Sands long enough that they trusted her. Still, whoever ran the Galaxy must have friends in high places. The club had been raided a few times, and each time the police had found no evidence at all –

someone must be tipping them off in advance. Mia said the building was owned by a syndicate, but she hadn't been able to find out much about that. There were layers upon layers of trusts and shady businesses that protected the name of the owner. Or owners.

'One of my sources did give me a name, though,' Mia had told him. 'The guy who runs the drug ring is called Mr White. He doesn't know the guy's first name, but that's what everyone calls him.'

He'd laughed when Mia told him that. Mr White. That had to be a play on Walter White, from *Breaking Bad*. Of course. They'd laughed about that at dinner. But now, just in case, he racked his brains to see if he knew anyone called White. He couldn't think of a single person he knew, either personally or professionally, with the last name White. Still, it could be worth checking out. He'd ask Rachel to check through their client files to see if they'd ever dealt with a Mr White. Maybe an old client, or someone they'd beaten to a deal on some property in the past?

Logically, the person behind all of this was Brian. Delaying Jason's project would benefit Brian's project. He'd asked Mia if Brian had anything to do with the Galaxy, but she had just shrugged and said, 'Not that I know of.' Something in his gut told him Brian was too lazy to construct an elaborate plot like this. The vandalism. The weird messages that linked back to his childhood. Still, he'd known Brian for a long time. Brian would know a lot of things about his past.

Jason put the thoughts out of his mind. Until he knew all the details, it wasn't worth rehashing over and over. He'd just have to find Frank and put some more pressure on him to uncover who was behind all this. But for now, he had to check out the site. He had an uncomfortable feeling that all was not right.

The building site was in darkness, apart from the streetlights. As soon as he pulled up, he could see that one of the security gates at the front of the complex was swinging open. *Shit*. That wasn't right. It should all still be locked up. No-one should be here this early. He checked his phone. It was 2.35 in the morning. He'd taken Frank's site key yesterday afternoon, but he could have made a copy. In fact, he probably had. Jason kicked himself for not changing all the locks on the site right away.

Jason parked the car and closed the door quietly behind him. He let himself in through the open gate. Inside, the site was perfectly still; everything neatly ordered and ready for the workers to get back into it as soon as Riggs gave them the go-ahead. It was a dark night, and the glow of the streetlights wasn't enough to banish the shadows. Jason headed for the front door, reaching for his keys. He tried the handle and the door opened. Yeah, something was definitely wrong.

He went inside. The building was eerily quiet and very dark. He was used to it being full of the sounds of drills and nail guns, tradies shouting to each other, and machinery reverberating outside. The absolute stillness made the hair on the back of his neck stand on end. But something made him pause. There *was* a noise there – the sound of voices somewhere in the building. Could it be an illusion? Someone walking down the street sounding like they were in the building? He didn't think so. He turned on his phone's torch – he'd asked Inga to show him how – and walked quietly toward the voices. The thin beam of light didn't do much to light up the inside of the building. Still, it wasn't hard to follow the distant sound of voices throughout the shell of the building. As he walked, the voices got louder. It sounded like an argument, then a fight. Then, in the midst of the shouting, a gunshot rang out.

———

On instinct, Jason ran toward the noise. He leapt up the concrete steps that led to the second floor, taking them two at a time, and out into the second-floor foyer. He could hear what sounded like two sets of footsteps running toward him. He stepped back into the shadows, turned off his torch, and waited. The only light coming into the foyer was from the streetlight outside the window.

After a few seconds, two men burst through a doorway, coming from one of the unfinished apartments. Jason could feel all his senses on high alert, his blood rushing in his ears. One of the men must have a gun. But he wasn't letting them get away. They both slowed to a walk, turning in the direction of the stairwell, and Jason sprang. He swept his foot out and kicked the legs out from under the first man, who crashed onto the floor with a grunt. Jason stepped forward and swung a left hook toward the second man's face. His knuckles connected and he felt the man's head snap backward. He staggered backward but caught his balance and stepped toward Jason, swinging wildly. Jason managed to dodge the swings and landed a solid punch to the guy's stomach.

He could hear the second man on the floor, scrabbling to get up. A distant part of his brain was screaming that one of them must have a gun. But the other part of his brain, the part that was raging, was firmly in control. He put his head down and charged toward the standing man, catching him just under the rib cage and knocking him flat on his back. The other man had made it to his feet, wheezing as the air had been knocked out of him. Jason swung around fast, just in time to block the punch that the shorter man was aiming for his face. But the guy was quick, and obviously had some kind of martial arts training, because he pivoted sideways and kicked, catching Jason's knee and sending him staggering backward.

Part of Jason's brain was still screaming a warning about the gun. But he wasn't afraid of it. If he was going out, he'd do it fighting, not running with his tail between his legs. His knee felt like jelly, but thanks to the adrenaline, he couldn't feel any pain. Yet. He stepped forward as the little guy sprang, and blocked a flurry of punches, once again thanking his brothers for his quick reflexes. He could see the other man in his peripheral vision, pushing himself to his feet. Jason knew he was about to face an attack from both men at the same time. The smaller guy looked toward his friend, distracted for a millisecond. It was all Jason needed. He darted forward and struck, feeling the man's nose crunch under his fist. Blood started pouring from it.

'Come on Tony, let's get the fuck out of here,' the smaller guy said, clutching at his bleeding nose. Jason moved to block their exit down the stairwell, but his injured knee slowed him down. The two men were younger and faster. They darted down the stairs, disappearing with a clatter of feet. Jason thought about following, but his knee – and the thought of the gunshot he'd heard – gave him pause. He wasn't going to catch them either way. And he still hadn't found Frank, which was why he was there in the first place. Instead, he turned toward the entrance the two men had come through and pushed open the heavy door to the unfinished apartment. He walked in through the corridor, past the kitchen and bathroom and into the living area.

It was absolute carnage. Someone had smashed at the plasterboard walls. Pipes and wiring lay broken and scattered against the wall and red paint had been splashed everywhere. In the middle of the destruction was a disaster worse than all that. Jason felt as though he'd been punched in the gut. Right there in front of him was a body, spread-eagled on the floor, lying in a pool of dark liquid. He turned the torch light in that direction. It was definitely blood, and a lot of it. *Fuck.* He was pretty sure he knew who it was, but just to be sure, he stepped closer. His worst suspicions were confirmed. It was Frank. He was lifeless and pale, with a bloody gunshot wound in the side of his head. In his right hand was a handgun. So that's where the gunfire had come from.

Jason felt the now-familiar sense that something wasn't right. He knew what it looked like. Frank had broken in and caused all this devastation, and then killed himself. But it just didn't seem right. For starters, there had been the other two guys, and the shouted argument. Why had they been here? And why the fuck was there red paint everywhere? Jason sidestepped the pool of blood and looked around the room. Ah. There it was. Along one wall in dripping red letters, was a message. *Think you're too good to wear the uniform? You're not the fucking captain.*

Jason felt the simmering anger in his gut boil over. This was absolutely personal, and he was done with it. Some absolute fucker messing with his project, causing him all kinds of delays was one thing. But now a man was dead. Not just any man, but Frank. His foreman, and his mate. Sure, Frank might have gotten himself into this somehow. He'd obviously made some mistakes, but that was no reason for him to wind up dead. The rage in his veins was white-hot now. Fuck, someone was going to have to tell Sandra. She would be devastated. Not only that, but whoever was behind all this, this bastard, this evil prick, was messing with his *kids*. Having them followed. The rage pouring through him solidified into determination. He was going to find whoever was behind all of this and stop him. No matter what it took.

———

Riggs was at the building site within fifteen minutes of his phone call, sirens blaring. She had two squad cars full of cops with her. They cordoned off the site while Jason led Riggs and her partner, the tall guy with the crew cut, to where the body lay. Jason watched her face, but Riggs didn't flinch as she looked down on the gruesome scene.

She looked up at Jason. 'Looks like your buddy Frank decided he'd have one more go at vandalising the site before he killed himself. Seems like he really had it in for you.'

'Right. That's what it looks like. But that's not what happened,' Jason insisted.

'Oh?' Riggs's eyebrows rose even further.

Jason remembered what had felt wrong when he first saw the dead body. 'Gun's in his right hand. Frank was left-handed.'

'Huh.' Riggs looked back at the body. 'Well, I guess you've still got the cameras operating. We'll be able to check out the footage.'

'Not likely.' Jason pointed to a corner of the room where a video camera had been wrenched off the wall and smashed to pieces on the floor. There was a camera on the landing where he'd fought off the two goons, though, so he was hoping there'd be some good footage there. Some way to identify them both.

Riggs frowned and made a note in her notepad. One of the other detectives had pulled out a camera and was taking photos of the scene. She looked up at the wall. 'What about this? Strange thing to graffiti on the wall. Does it make any sense to you?'

Jason nodded, gritting his teeth. 'Yep. I know exactly what that means. And it's clearly directed at me.'

CHAPTER 15

n high school, Jason hadn't given a shit about popularity. He had his gang of friends, the same guys he'd been hanging out with since those early days running around Woodridge, and he didn't need anything else. He didn't care what anyone at school thought of him, either. Turned out that was one of the essential components of being popular – the absolute refusal to give a shit. Somehow, Jason had figured out the code without even trying. And so as he progressed through high school, Jason found, much to his surprise, that he was popular. Not that he really cared. He didn't give a shit about being a cool kid. It just meant that his gang of friends had more hangers-on. More desperate, pimply-faced boys who thought they might get popular just by being close to him.

There were a few things that Jason *did* care about in high school, though. The first and most important thing was having fun. He'd lost count of the number of times he was kicked out of class for acting the fool, playing pranks on other kids or making jokes that would have the whole class in stiches and the teacher tearing at his hair in frustration. Lunch and recess were spent eating as much food as he could – he was a growing boy, after all – and then coming up with more pranks and high jinks. Or maybe they'd just kick the footy back and forward across the oval, shouting insults at each other and leaping up to take marks off each other's shoulders.

The other thing he cared about was making money. He'd been the child of a single mother, and pocket money had always been something other kids got. Money was just in such short supply, even though his mum made sure they never went without anything. Now that she had married again, he and his brothers had regular, if modest, pocket money. But it wasn't enough. He wanted more. Or maybe his natural ability as an entrepreneur was starting to assert itself. He started out by buying bags of lollies at the corner shop and selling them off individually to the sugar-craving kids at school. He worked out that he could buy a fifty-cent bag of mixed lollies, then sell each of those lollies for five cents, making a tidy profit. As puberty started to hit the kids at school hard, he worked out he could make a tonne more money by buying bootleg porn and copying it onto VCR tapes. One of his brothers helped him to work out how to do it using a spare recorder they borrowed from one of their friends. There was so much demand he couldn't keep up with it. He learned a lot about supply and demand in those high school days. Better than any economics class.

As high school dragged on interminably, he started to care about something else as well. He was sick and tired of being treated like a little kid and wanted to be taken seriously. He'd be seventeen soon – old enough to get a job and support his family. Old enough to drive. Nearly old enough to vote or get married. Not that he wanted to do either of those things any time soon. But these teachers treated him as though he was barely capable of wiping his own arse just because he didn't pay attention in class or spend much time on his homework. Well, he never did any homework, that was for sure. But he was already making plenty of money by then, running all kinds of schemes and little backyard businesses. He didn't need calculus or English literature or biology to be successful. He was going to be successful anyway.

In Year 12, when the elections for school captain came up, Jason threw his name in the ring as a joke. Just being his usual larrikin self. But, if he was being honest, there was a tiny bit of a *fuck you* to all the teachers who didn't take him seriously. He made speeches along with all the other candidates, and even though he didn't prepare in advance, he got the most resounding response of all the nominees. He'd always been a natural-born performer. A big part of his platform was that if he was elected captain, he'd abolish the school uniform. It was a horrible, ugly thing. White shirts that were supposed to be ironed but were worn as wrinkled as a grandpa's ass by most kids, itchy grey pants, and a tie that Jason usually wore knotted around his head. He was always in trouble for not wearing the uniform properly and, of course, his mates followed suit. His hand-drawn campaign posters read Vote for Jason, and featured a picture of his head, tie around it ninja style.

In the end he didn't win the election, although he strongly suspected that the principal, who was responsible for counting the votes, had altered the results. A preppy, smart-assed kid who not many people liked was declared school captain. Jason couldn't even remember what his name was. Something like Christopher or Wilbur. Then, in the weeks that followed, Jason's friends started referring to him as the school captain anyway. It started out as a joke but by the end of the year, most of the kids at school genuinely believed that Jason was school captain. He even got called on by a few of the teachers to shake hands with visiting dignitaries and hand out certificates to some of the lower-school kids. He thought it was a fantastic joke. He knew that the principal, and a few of the other kids – probably including Wilbur or Christopher or whatever his name was – were pissed off at him, but he truly couldn't have cared less. The whole thing of picking a captain was a stupid tradition anyway, just designed to give one preppy nerd a giant ego and make the rest of the school feel inferior.

When school finished, it didn't matter anyway. In the real world, it didn't matter if you were popular in high school or not, whether you got good grades, or whether you were the school captain. All those things didn't make a difference when you were out in the big wide world. In Jason's mind, it was just a funny story he and his friends joked about when they remembered those crazy high school days. But he wasn't one of those people who thought your popularity or success at school meant you'd be successful and popular in the real world. He didn't care much about that either. He just wanted to enjoy his life and make some cold, hard cash. As much as he possibly could.

———

Jason let the memories rush over him as he stood in the vandalised building, Frank's dead body still lay in a pool of blood on the floor. Riggs stood with her notebook out, listening to his story. Around them, technicians in protective white suits with plastic booties over their shoes photographed every inch of the room. They'd brought big lights with them, which were now set up around the room, illuminating the space. Outside, the early morning sky was still dark.

'So you think this message on the wall is related to this incident from high school?' Riggs asked, the scepticism heavy in her voice.

'Yeah, I do. Which means that whoever did this is someone I know. Someone who has known me since high school.' He thought back to the previous messages. 'Well, primary school, actually. They're trying to send me a message, although what the hell that message is, I can't think.'

Riggs squinted at him and made a note in her little book. 'So, no idea who it might be? Could it be the kid who was elected school captain? Christopher?'

Jason shrugged. 'No idea. I'm sure it wasn't him though. I think he's living overseas somewhere, last I heard. Or I could have the wrong guy, I barely remember him.' He shrugged. 'I still don't know who's behind this. But I'm sure as hell going to figure it out.'

'What about the other developer, Brian? You thought it might be him.'

Jason pondered this for a minute. He could see Brian having some kind of vindictive grudge against him, but honestly, the guy was far too lazy to go this far. And he was almost certainly too much of a coward to kill someone. 'I don't think it's Brian,' he told Riggs. 'Plus, I only met him after high school. He wasn't there for all this.'

Riggs frowned. 'But you and your mates chat about high school. He could have heard you talking about the school captain thing.'

'Yeah, sure, he could have.' Jason gestured toward the red paint on the wall. 'But this feels personal. Whoever wrote this was actually there.' There had been about 600 kids at his high school – not a particularly big school, but a lot of suspects.

Riggs closed her notebook and tapped on the plastic cover with her pen. She cleared her throat. 'You realise you're a suspect as well, right Jason? Why were you here in the middle of the night? You could have easily interrupted Frank in the act of vandalising your building site and shot him yourself. Look, you've got blood all over you, too.'

Jason glanced down at his blood-splattered shirt and at his knuckles, which were also bloody. 'Yeah, that's not Frank's blood. It belongs to one of the goons I interrupted when I got here. You can test it if you want to.' He went to take off his shirt, but Riggs stopped him.

'We can just swab your hand.' She waved one of the techs over. He swabbed Jason's knuckles and bagged the sample. 'Even if it's not Frank's blood, that doesn't prove your innocence. Do you own a gun, Jason?'

Jason laughed at the absurdity of the idea. He was a lover, not a fighter. 'No, I don't. Never have. And, like I told you, I came here because of the phone call from Frank's wife.'

She nodded. 'Do you have anyone who can verify your whereabouts last night? Up until this phone call?'

Jason remembered waking up next to Mia. 'It just so happens I was with a beautiful woman all night last night, Riggs. Right up until Frank's wife phoned me and dragged me out of bed.'

'Okay. I'm going to need her number to confirm your alibi.'

'Sure.' Jason was sick of this conversation already. There was a man dead on the floor in front of him – a man he'd considered a friend – and Riggs was wasting time on the ridiculous theory that he would vandalise his own site and murder his own foreman.

'And you realise we're going to need to shut the site down.'

It was the last thing he cared about. 'Of course. I don't give a shit about the building project right now. My friend is dead. Do what you need to do.'

'And I'm going to need to bring you into the station to ask a few questions.'

It was the last straw. 'For fuck's sake, Riggs. Why the fuck are you wasting your time on trying to prove that for some fucking reason, I'd do this to my own site? And a man who was my friend? You can ask me whatever questions you want. I'm an open book. Check the security tapes, they'll back me up. But, while you're doing that, I'm going to find the killer.' He turned on his heels and walked away.

———

Jason drove home from the site with waves of rage pulsing through him. Frank was dead. Any time now, Sandra would be getting a knock on the door from a disinterested police officer who would very politely inform her that her husband was dead. Jason had wanted to do it himself. He felt that he owed that to Sandra – to Frank – but Riggs had told him that would be a breach of protocol. And, as angry as he was with her right now, Jason knew the detective was just doing her job. As far as he could tell, she was a good cop. She was uptight as hell, but she seemed to give a shit about doing things the right way. So, he'd agreed not to contact Sandra until the officer had delivered the bad news. He'd go and see her that afternoon.

He was furious at Frank. Not that it mattered now. But if Frank had simply trusted him enough to come and tell him he was being blackmailed, they wouldn't be in this situation. And if Frank had told him everything, they would have been able to work out a plan that would keep him safe. And alive.

The thought that was gnawing at him more than anything else was that whoever had murdered Frank was also following his kids around. It sent a new wave of violent anger pulsing through him. There was no way in hell he was going to let anything happen to his kids. He was going to find whoever this asshole was and tear him limb from limb before he let a single thing happen to his kids.

First, though, he needed to work out who was behind all of this. He had all the pieces now, he was sure. But the rage in his system was clouding his thoughts. He had to calm his mind and think through all of the pieces of the puzzle. He'd be able to work it out. So Jason turned his car toward the place that calmed him and helped him to concentrate. The place where he felt most at peace. The beach.

CHAPTER 16

By the time Jason got to the beach, the sun was just starting to rise. He watched the rays of golden sunlight creeping over the horizon and the little waves rolling into the shore. The beach was starting to fill with early morning joggers, dog walkers and swimmers. It was another spectacular day at Golden Sands, and yet the beauty was wasted on him. All he could think about was Frank's body, lying in that pool of blood on the floor. *Fuck.* He couldn't believe that Frank was dead. He'd known Frank for years, they'd worked together well, most of the time at least. And now he was gone. He thought of Sandra, and of how devastated she would be. *Shit.* He'd have to go see her. He'd do it that morning.

Even more troubling than the thought that Frank was dead was that the murderer was still out there. He had no doubt it had been murder. And the murderer had it in for him. And knew who his kids were, and where they worked. Again, rage filled his body. Whoever this bastard was, Jason was going to take him down. He'd never felt more determined about anything.

But first, he needed a coffee. Badly. He also wanted to check in with his kids and make sure they were both okay. And remind them to be careful. Just until he'd dealt with this murderous asshole. He should also probably talk to Mia. The thought of Mia filled his body with warmth as he remembered the night before. Yeah, he really needed to talk to Mia and make sure she knew that he wanted to see her again. And soon.

Jason could see a coffee van parked just a couple hundred metres up the beach from where he was sitting on a little stone retaining wall at the edge of the sand. The van had a steady stream of customers lining up to get their morning caffeine fix. Just what he needed. As he stood and started to walk down the beach, spikes of pain radiated from his knee up his leg. Shit. He must have really damaged it when the asshole wannabe ninja kicked him in the knee. He'd also have to pay a visit to his physio this morning, so she could tape it up and make it at least functional for now. He'd deal with it properly later. Jason hobbled the rest of the way down to the coffee van, feeling older than he really was, and bought himself the largest coffee they had.

———

By the time he reached Sandra's house, Jason had finished the giant coffee and felt much better. He'd also phoned both his kids – thank God they were both early risers – and they'd both assured him they were fine and would be careful. Sandra's house was in a suburb about half an hour's drive across town. Jason had been there just the day before, but he'd already forgotten the address and had to ask Rachel to send it to him. What would he do without her? Rachel had told him she was on her way to the office to meet with Riggs and show her the security camera footage. At least that was one thing he didn't have to do. He'd had just about enough of Detective Riggs for now.

Sandra's house was a plain, slightly drab townhouse with a lawn that needed a mow. Jason thought with a start that Frank wouldn't be around to do that anymore. He made a mental note to come around with a lawnmower and do it for her. Not that he owned a lawnmower – he usually paid someone to do that job. He'd get his regular guy to come around and do it. That was a better idea. Jason walked up the front path and knocked. Sandra opened the door within seconds. Her face was tear-stained, and when she saw Jason, she dissolved into fresh tears. He stepped forward and folded her into a big hug. Sandra sobbed onto his shoulder for a few minutes. Then she stepped back. 'I'm so glad you've come, Jason. Come and sit down.'

Jason followed her into the little lounge room with its faded couches. 'I'm so sorry, Sandra. I wish I knew what to say, but there's just no words.'

She sighed. 'I knew this day might come. He'd been mixed up with some of the worst people, and he owed them money. He was such a terrible gambler. Always gambled more than he could afford, and always lost.'

'He was a good foreman. I want you to know that, Sandra. I'm grateful I got to work with him. Sorry it ended like this.' He paused. He didn't want to have to ask her questions about Frank's situation, but he needed to know. 'Is there anything that you can tell me about the men that Frank owed money to?' Jason asked.

Sandra shrugged. 'Not really. He didn't talk about it, you know? Just every now and again when he was drunk or really scared.' She paused for a moment. 'He did mention one name a few times. A man called Mr White. I got the impression he was the boss. Frank was really scared of him.'

Jason tensed. Mr White again. 'Did he mention anything else about this guy, Mr White?'

She shook her head. 'No. Although I think he was in the drug business. He was running some kind of drug dealing ring out of some nightclub in Golden Sands.'

'The Galaxy?' Jason asked. It seemed like it really was an open secret. He was pissed off no-one had had the decency to tell him earlier on.

Sandra looked up. 'Yeah, that could be it. Frank mentioned it one night when he was rambling about something. Said he had to go to the Galaxy to give some money to someone. Maybe Mr White. I was really upset because we had to pay our rent, and he kept saying if he didn't give Mr White what he owed him, it would be curtains for him. He seemed really scared.'

Jason nodded. 'Okay, thanks Sandra. That's helpful.'

'I just don't understand why he had to pull you into this.' Sandra rubbed at her face, looking like she'd aged a decade since Jason last saw her.

'Yeah, I'm not sure either, Sandra. This guy Mr White seems to have it in for me, but I don't know why. Judging from some of the graffiti he's left at my building, he's someone I knew when I was a kid. But I haven't been able to work out who it is yet.'

'And Frank just happened to owe him money?'

'Yeah. Or he knew Frank was my foreman and bought his debt off someone else. I think that's more likely,' Jason said.

Sandra was quiet for a while, and Jason decided it was time to go. He gave her another hug before he left. 'Now Sandra, you let me know if you need anything, won't you? Anything at all.' He made a promise to himself that he would look after her. It was the least he could do for Frank.

———

The rest of the morning was taken up by going to the physio to get his knee strapped and fielding some more questions from Riggs. She'd obviously decided against arresting him for Frank's murder right away, but she told him in no uncertain terms that he was still a suspect. As soon as he had time, Jason stopped at a florist and bought a huge bunch of red roses. He'd decided against phoning Mia. He'd rather see her in person. As he got into the car to drive to her office, his phone rang. It was an unfamiliar number. Normally he'd ignore a call like that, but just in case it was to do with the killing, he answered.

'Hello, is that Jason?' the voice sounded like a child playing a prank. He almost hung up, but something made him pause.

'Yes. Who's this?'

'It's Stella. We met at the Galaxy.' Again, the voice was childlike.

For a moment, Jason couldn't place who she was. His head was filled with thoughts of Frank's murder and the mess at the building site.

She continued on. 'You stepped in when one of the guys was threatening me and, um, you gave me your business card. You said to call if I ever needed help.' Jason could hear the hint of tears in her voice. In a rush, the memory of the night at the Galaxy with Pauly came back to him.

'Right, yeah, I remember.' Of course he did. 'Are you okay? Do you need help?'

'Yeah.' Her voice was hesitant, and she seemed fearful. 'I don't really want to talk over the phone. Can we meet in person?'

Jason felt a sense of hesitation. His gut was telling him it wasn't a good idea. But she was a girl in distress. Something about her reminded him of his own daughter. What else could he say? 'Yes, sure. Where can I meet you?'

'Um, near the Galaxy? There's a little laneway down the side of the building. Maybe there?'

Jason knew the place. 'Sure. When?'

'I'll be there in an hour.'

Jason checked his phone. He could see Mia and still make it there in an hour. 'Okay. I'll meet you there.'

'Thank you,' the relief in her voice was mingled with an emotion more like fear. 'Oh, and could you come alone?'

Sure, thought Jason, I'll come alone to meet someone I don't know at all, who might be associated with someone who's been trying to destroy my business and who recently murdered my foreman. But instead of arguing with her, he said, 'I'll see you in an hour, Stella.'

At Mia's office, the receptionist waved Jason in. Mia was sitting behind her desk, working at her computer with a frown on her face. When she saw Jason, she smiled. *God, she was a beautiful woman.* He placed the roses on her desk and came around to where she was sitting. Mia stood to greet him. He pulled her to him and kissed her, slowly and deeply. The memory of last night was still fresh, although so much had happened since then that it seemed like a hundred years ago.

'You had to run off pretty early this morning,' she said, smiling up at him. 'I wasn't sure I'd see you again. Is everything okay?'

'No, not really.' Jason sat on the edge of her desk and told her all about the fight with the two goons at his building site and then finding

Frank's dead body. Her eyes widened, but she listened without showing any other reaction. 'I'm a suspect, as you can imagine,' he explained. 'But we've got cameras set up throughout the building, so that should corroborate my story. Even if the goons have smashed a couple of them.'

Concern filled Mia's eyes. 'It sounds like someone's really got it in for you, Jason. I'm worried about you.'

He laughed. 'Don't worry about me. But whoever is behind all this should be worried, that's for sure. I've got another lead.' He filled her in on the details of the phone call from Stella. 'I'm hoping she might be able to tell me a bit more about this mysterious Mr White that everyone's so scared of.' He checked his watch. 'I've got to get going soon. She said she'd meet me in the alley near the Galaxy.'

'You're not going to meet with her, are you? It sounds like a trap to me.' She'd put words to the feeling that was still swirling in his gut.

'Yeah, I know. Sounds like a trap to me, too. But don't worry, I can take care of myself. Anyone who's trying to trap me will find out that's not such an easy thing to do.'

CHAPTER 17

The alley near the Galaxy was narrow, with three big skip bins lined up along one side. One was overflowing with cardboard boxes and one was filled to the brim with black bags of rubbish, so the lids wouldn't shut properly. The third bin was propped open, the smell of rotting vegetables emanating from it. The alley ran down between two buildings, the Galaxy on one side and a Chinese restaurant on the other. The tall structures blocked out the afternoon sunlight. Past the bulk of the Galaxy, Jason could see the alley continue on between the next two buildings, closed off by a tall fence topped with barbed wire.

Jason was a few minutes early, but as his eyes adjusted to the dim light, he saw what he was expecting. There was a small figure down the end of the alley, standing in front of the barbed wire fence. Stella, he guessed. Of course she was right down the end of the alley, and there were no other exits from the narrow space. He stepped into the alley and walked toward her, taking a careful note of his surroundings. The Chinese restaurant was made of brown brick and the windows at the back of the building were covered in mesh. The one door on that side was padlocked. The Galaxy was also brick, but those bricks had been painted a deep steel grey, obviously long enough ago that parts of the paintwork were chipped and peeling, showing the red brick underneath. The one doorway into the Galaxy was about halfway down the alley. Beside it was a small window with a frayed curtain pulled over it. Jason deliberately didn't look at the window as he passed.

Stella was standing hunched over, looking down at the ground. She was small, probably shorter than Inga, and she was wearing an oversized black hoodie. As he approached she glanced up at him, and he could see her face was tear-stained. As he expected.

'I'm sorry,' she whispered when he was close enough to hear. 'They made me call you here.'

'Yeah. I thought as much.' He stood next to her, but turned his body to the side so he could glance down the alley behind him. 'So we don't have much time, do we?'

She looked up at him. 'What do you mean?'

'They'll be here any minute, won't they? So I need you to tell me now. What is Mr White's real name? I can help you, Stella, but you've got to help me.'

She kept her eyes on him, her face filled with fear. For a moment, he thought she was going to cry. 'I can't...' she started.

'Stella, I've got a daughter your age. They're stalking her. I need to put a stop to all of this but I can't if I don't know who I'm fighting.'

At that moment, there was a screech of rusty hinges and a beam of light shone from the doorway to the Galaxy. The light was blocked out as one man stepped out into the alley, then another. The second man slammed the door behind him. The afternoon sunlight behind them turned both men into silhouettes, and Jason could see the clear outline of a gun in the larger man's hand. They both had their eyes fixed on him as they stood side by side, blocking the alley as though they expected him to run. *Wrong, fuckers*, Jason thought. *I'm not going anywhere.*

In one smooth motion, Jason stepped behind Stella, grabbing her arm with one hand while he pulled a knife from the sheath at his hip with the other. He held the knife in front of her, level with her neck. Normally, he would never even dream of threatening a woman like this, but his mind filled with pictures of Frank lying dead in a pool of blood. He had been messed up, he'd made plenty of mistakes, but

Frank was his *friend*. He was not going to let that slide. He'd do exactly what he had to do to make things right, find out who this fucker was, and keep his family safe.

The two men in the alley seemed alarmed by him grabbing Stella. They'd obviously expected fight or flight from him. They glanced at each other, and didn't seem to know what to do.

'I'm not going to hurt you,' Jason whispered in Stella's ear. 'I just need these goons to drop the gun.'

On cue, the bigger man lifted the gun and pointed it at him. 'Let the girl go. She doesn't mean anything to us. We just want to talk to you.'

Jason almost laughed. Sure they just wanted to talk. It was the two guys he'd run into at the building site the night he'd found Frank's body, he was sure of it. One of them still had a black eye. And he was betting on one thing – the girl had a connection to the big boss that was behind whatever this operation was. He didn't exactly know who she was to him, but he was about to find out.

The two goons looked nervous. 'Let the girl go, or we'll shoot her,' one of them shouted.

Jason grinned at them. 'Yeah, I bet you won't. In fact, I'm betting that if this girl gets a single scratch on her, you'll both be in huge trouble. I think she's someone important to your boss, isn't she?' He thought for a moment. Not the boss's girlfriend. She was too young, not glamorous enough. 'She's his daughter, isn't she?' he called. The look of alarm that passed between the two goons confirmed his suspicions. Stella glanced up at him in surprise. Yep. He was on the right track. Jason let them sweat for a few moments, pointing the knife at the girl's neck with careful attention.

'I don't want to hurt her, but I will if I have to. I'm guessing you don't want that. So, here's what we're going to do,' he called to the two men standing in the alley. 'You throw your gun in the skip bin, and I'll let the girl go. And then we'll settle this like men. Just between us. I'll take the two of you on at once, just so it's a fair fight,' he taunted.

Again, he noticed the look that passed between them. They stepped in toward each other and had a quick, whispered conversation, obviously working out what to do. Jason took the opportunity to lean toward Stella and speak quietly to her. 'You're his daughter, aren't you?' The girl glanced up at him again, and he could see by the look on her face that he was right. Jason felt a moment of disgust that this Mr White would use his own daughter as bait to get back at him. He also felt sorry for the poor girl. He bent toward her ear again. 'In a moment, those goons are going to ditch their gun, and then you're going to run out of here as fast as you can. And not look back. But before that, I need you to tell me Mr White's real name. Now.' There was a note of menace in his voice.

Stella hesitated. The two men stepped back into formation, but he could see they'd made a decision. 'Okay. We'll do it,' the larger man shouted. 'But you have to let her go first.' He held the gun out at arm's length.

Jason laughed. 'No. I'm not letting her go until the gun is in the dumpster. Now, how much trouble do you think you'd be in if I give her a scar?' He held the knife to the girl's face. She didn't tremble, obviously trusting him to keep his word about not hurting her.

The two men looked panicked. 'Okay, okay. Look. Gun in the bin. Then you let her go, right?' The man holding the gun stepped toward the open skip bin, holding the gun out toward it.

'Yes, that's right,' Jason nodded. He was betting on the fact these two assholes only had one gun between them. If the smaller guy had one he'd already be holding it. Jason was willing to bet the other guy's gun was the one they'd left in Frank's hand. He lent toward Stella's ear. 'Stella, I need that name, now.'

Her lips barely moved as she said the words. 'His real name is Richard Whitten.'

Jason felt a shock of recognition, but before he could think any more about it, the goon with the gun stepped toward the skip bin and dropped it in. The sound of the gun falling into the bin was muffled by the rubbish at the bottom. Jason could see the panic on both men's faces.

He pushed Stella forward. 'Run, Stella. Go home and don't look back.' The girl gave a yelp of alarm, but she did as he said, skittering past the two men in the alley and disappearing from view around the Galaxy's corner. The men turned to make sure she'd made it to safety, and Jason made his move. There were two of them and only one of him, and he'd need the element of surprise. He ran down the alley as fast as his injured knee could carry him and let his momentum propel him into the smaller man. The guy was shorter than Jason but built like the proverbial brick shithouse. Still, thanks to his years of playing rugby and growing up with brothers, Jason had a solid tackle. The guy went over like a bag of cement, landing heavily on one shoulder. The taller man had swung into action by now, charging toward Jason. The knife was still in Jason's hand and he held it out, making the bigger guy stop his advance.

'Fuck. Jerry, get up here and help me,' he called to the guy who was scrambling his way up from the ground, holding his shoulder. Jason knew he only had a moment before both of them would be on him, and even though he had a knife, he didn't think those were good odds. He lunged forward, swiping at the bigger guy's arm with the knife. Both men wore T-shirts and jeans, and the bigger guy was wearing a hat that shaded his face. As well as both obviously having a thing for steroids, each also had a sleeve of tattoos on one arm. The bigger guy had a tattoo on his neck. Jason couldn't quite make it out, but it was possibly a dragon.

A line of blood opened up along the man's arm where Jason had nicked him with the knife. He stepped back, out of knife range, and pulled a set of brass knuckles from his pocket.

'What do you assholes want?' Jason yelled, keeping the big man at bay with the knife while keeping his eye on Jerry, who was still pulling himself upright.

The guy with the dragon neck tattoo spat on the ground. 'Jerry wants revenge for where you clocked him the other night,' he sneered. 'And then Mr White wants us to teach you a lesson.'

'Yeah? And what lesson is that?' Jason asked. He was circling Dragon Neck now, keeping away from Jerry, who was still holding his shoulder.

'The lesson is to keep off our turf. He doesn't take kindly to you showing up around here with your big plans and arrogant attitude. You especially need to stay away from the girl.' With that, the man charged at him, ducking under Jason's knife swipe and swinging at his jaw with the brass knuckles. Jason dodged, and then stabbed at the man's shoulder. He didn't want to kill the guy, just incapacitate him. He made contact, but only enough to make him flinch and roar with anger. 'Grab him, Jerry. Get that fucking knife off him.'

Jason easily dodged out of Jerry's way and aimed a kick at Dragon Neck. He made contact with the guy's hip, knocking him off balance. Then he swung a punch with his left hand, feeling the guy's cheekbone under his fist.

The bigger guy was disoriented now, and Jason stepped forward ready to finish him off. A knife through somewhere that was non-life-threatening but would still stop him from moving was the goal. But in the flurry of activity he'd lost track of Jerry, who'd found an iron bar on the ground, probably fallen from one of the Chinese restaurant's disintegrating windows. The bar hit Jason across the hand and he dropped the knife. He shouted with pain. *Fuck.* That had been his one advantage. He channelled his rage and swung around to punch Jerry in the face with his other hand, connecting squarely with Jerry's already bruised eye. It was not Jerry's day. Then Jason swung back and charged at Dragon Neck, shoving him backward into the skip bin with a thunderous clang.

The noise from the alley was obviously attracting attention. Jason could hear shouts and the banging of windows from the apartments above the Chinese restaurant. It wouldn't be long before someone called the cops. Jason raised his fist to hit the Dragon Neck guy again, but as he swung, Jerry came up behind him, panting hard, and put an arm around Jason's throat. *Fuck.* That was exactly what Jason had wanted to avoid. Dragon Neck pushed away from the skip bin with a sneer on his face. 'We've got you where we want you now. Hold him, Jerry, I'm going to make him pay.' Blood trickled down his face and one eye was swollen shut. The cut on his arm was still dripping blood. He was panting hard, the dragon tattoo pulsing with each breath.

In the distance, Jason could hear a police siren. Instantly, the look on the man's face changed from a sneer to panic. He swung at Jason, hitting him square in the stomach. It winded him and he prepared himself for the next flurry of hits. He had to get out of this headlock. Drawing on all his childhood experience of scrapping and dirty fights, Jason leaned forward, pulling Jerry in toward him, and swung his head back hard, connecting with what was probably his nose. Jerry's arm around his neck instantly went slack, and Jason turned around in time to see him hit the deck, out cold. He turned back to Dragon Neck, who was rattled. It was one on one now, and Jason was ready to dish out a few punches. But with the wailing of the police siren getting closer, Dragon Neck turned and ran for the back door into the Galaxy, leaving his buddy out cold on the ground. The door clanged shut behind him just as a police car skidded to a stop at the entrance to the alley.

CHAPTER 18

As soon as the dust had cleared and the siren had stopped ringing in his ears, Jason pulled out his phone. The police officers were reading Jerry his rights before bundling him into the cruiser for a little holiday in a nice, comfortable cell. It was absolutely not that guy's day. He had another black eye and probably a broken nose, courtesy of the back of Jason's head.

Jason had given the young officers his statement, telling them how the two thugs had jumped him in the alley when he was just minding his own business, and luckily someone in an apartment over the Chinese restaurant had seen enough of the fight to corroborate his story. Jason told them about the vandalism at his building site, and Frank's murder, and he was pretty sure Jerry would be implicated in both those things too. A young cop, clearly the poor sap who'd drawn the short straw, was digging around in the skip bin to find the gun. Jason hadn't mentioned Stella in his statement – he didn't want the girl getting dragged into this whole mess; she had enough to deal with already.

Jason had gotten off pretty lightly, all things considered. He had a couple of new bruises, but since there had been both a knife and a gun in that alley and he'd been outnumbered two to one, he was grateful to still be in one piece. And, more importantly, he'd found out some important information, thanks to Stella. He turned over the name she'd told him in his mind. Richard Whitten. He was fairly sure he knew who that was. A giant piece of the puzzle falling into place. He dialled Pauly's number, just to be sure.

Pauly answered on the first ring. 'Hey, J man. How ya doing?'

Jason almost laughed. 'Well, considering I just got jumped in an alley by two guys with a gun, I'm surprisingly good.'

'What!' Pauly's voice filled with alarm. 'How did you get out of that one?'

This time, Jason *did* laugh. 'Let's just say that growing up with brothers and all that rough and tumble we used to do in the school playground came in handy. Oh, that and the fact I've got a hard head.'

'Oh, man, I'm so glad you're okay.'

'Hey Pauly, I need to ask you something. That kid who lived on our block when we were growing up, Richie someone or other. He had a swimming pool in his backyard, and he liked to boss us all around and make us act like little trained monkeys before he'd let us in his pool. Liked to pretend he was a big deal. Remember him?'

'Yeah. Yeah, I sure do. Little punk. He liked you more than me. I hardly ever got to swim in that pool.'

'Right. Do you remember his last name? Was it Whitten? Richard Whitten?'

Pauly thought for a moment. 'Yeah, I reckon that was it.'

'Huh. Well, I don't think he likes me anymore. I think he's the one behind all the damage at my building site. And Frank's murder.'

'Shit, no way! Really?'

'Yeah. What else do you know about him?'

Pauly sounded thoughtful. 'Not that much, really. Just, I remember hearing my mum talking about his mum once. Apparently his dad was a sadistic bastard, liked to beat his mum up from time to time. I don't think he ever laid a hand on Richie, though. He thought the sun shone out of that kid.'

'Yeah, I remember him at school one time when a bunch of us had gotten in trouble for something. I think we lit a rubbish bin on fire behind the gym, remember that? Well, his dad came in, guns blazing, shouting at the principal. He said his kid would never do anything like that. I was mad because we all got detention but Richie got let off.'

Pauly laughed at the memory. 'Yeah, that's right. I think his dad was pretty rich.' He spoke thoughtfully. 'You know, I heard some stuff about him after school. From some of the guys.'

'Yeah? What'd you hear? It could be helpful.' Jason knew the guys he and Pauly hung out with liked a good gossip from time to time.

'Just that he'd been implicated in some pretty shady shit. Drug deals, but not your usual street corner stuff. Like, he was a big kingpin or something. But nothing ever seemed to stick to him. He could afford the best lawyers, of course, so he always got away with things.'

'Yeah. That sounds about right. I wonder why he's got it in for me?'

'Oh, that's easy,' Pauly said. 'He always wanted to be popular, but no-one liked him. Mostly because he was a bossy, arrogant little prick. He was jealous of you because everyone liked you.'

It made sense. Jason could imagine Richie, an adult now, but still full of festering resentment at those who'd been more popular than he was. And then Jason had unknowingly bought the property down the road from the Galaxy, which was probably the centre of his drug distribution ring. And that had triggered the vandalism and attacks on his building. 'Yeah, maybe you're right, Pauly. I guess the cryptic messages make sense now. It was Richie trying to send some kind of message. Thanks Pauly, appreciate your help.'

'Don't mention it, man. Just watch your back, hey? Sounds like the little prick is batshit crazy.'

Jason felt uneasy. Should he have seen this coming? He'd always been easy going and friendly enough that people generally liked him. Had he done something to make Richie hate him? He honestly didn't think he'd thought of the kid once since they all went their separate ways after high school. Clearly Richie had spent plenty of time festering over old wounds, though.

He sifted back through memories of his childhood, picturing Richie as he was back then. He had been a cute kid. Blond, with big blue eyes. He'd always worn nice clothes to school and had the fanciest bike of all the kids in the neighbourhood, leading to the nickname Richie Rich. Jason remembered him being bossy and manipulative, trying to get kids to like him, using his toys and the swimming pool in his back yard. Jason didn't give a shit if Richie liked him or not, but he did like swimming in the pool, so he tried to keep on his good side.

In high school, Richie had not been that cute. His blond hair had darkened and was lank and greasy. He'd had bad acne and a set of braces that made him look like every teenager's worst nightmare. Still, Jason couldn't remember being mean to him, ever. He remembered that two kids had followed Richie everywhere, his two little shadows, despite the fact that Richie was actively mean to them every chance he got. Jason had always felt sorry for Richie's little minions. He remembered seeing Richie push one of them into a muddy ditch when they were walking home one day, and laughing cruelly. He thought now about Stella, and felt sorry for her too. He couldn't imagine Richie as a father, although of course a lot of years had passed since he was a pimply high-schooler.

It was because of Richie's vendetta against Jason that Frank was dead. Well, because of that and Frank's gambling habits. But still, could Jason have done something to stop this? He didn't know, and it was adding to his uneasy feeling. He was sure as hell going to put a stop to it now, though.

Jason walked back to his car. He felt like he was on autopilot, heading toward the one person who could help him make some sense of everything. His Nan Dooksie. The sharpness she'd had in her younger years had faded a bit, but she was still the wisest person he knew. He turned in the direction of her house and, before he knew it, was pulling up in her driveway.

Nan answered the door when he knocked, her wispy hair and wide blue eyes just the same as always. He gave her a big hug.

'Nan, it's always so good to see you.'

'You too, Jason. I wasn't expecting you, but it's always nice to have a visit from my favourite grandson.' Jason laughed. Nan called all of her grandchildren her favourites, but he secretly thought he really *was* her favourite. 'Is something the matter? Come in. Let me make you a cup of tea, and you can tell me all about it.'

Jason sat in his nan's kitchen while the kettle boiled and told her all about the events of the day, leaving out some of the more violent details. He told her about discovering who Richie was, and his realisation that his old school mate was behind the trail of destruction that had run through his life over the last few weeks. Nan listened to everything with her usual attention.

'So, what's worrying you, Jason?' she asked. 'You've solved the mystery, haven't you? Surely the police will be able to bring this Richie character to justice now?'

'Well, that's just it,' Jason said. 'He seems to be able to wriggle out of everything. Like Pauly said, he's been implicated in some pretty bad stuff before, but he's gotten away with it. He's got a tonne of money and really good lawyers.' He paused. 'That's not really what's bothering me, though. I'm just wondering if I should have seen this coming in some way, and stopped it. I don't think I was particularly mean to this kid in school. If anything, I ignored him. But for some reason, he's fixated on me.'

'Oh, Jason. You can't live your life worried that you might have accidentally upset someone. You've never worried about what other people think of you, and that's one of your most wonderful qualities.'

'You know, Nan, I've got some regrets about how I've lived my life. I drank too much when I was married to Susan. Said some things I shouldn't have. Got behind the wheel of the car when I shouldn't have been driving. But I've really been trying to make amends for those things. Now I'm wondering if I need to add another regret to my list.'

Nan shook her head. 'Of course not. You're not responsible for other people's actions. Don't be ridiculous.'

Jason laughed. Leave it to Nan to tell him the truth without mincing her words. And she was right. Of course he wasn't responsible for what some psychopath chose to do. Even if they did go to school together.

'Yeah, thanks Nan. You're right. Of course.' He realised that his feeling of unease came from a sense of responsibility for the people in his life. He cared about them, from his family right through to the crew that worked for him. And this Richie was putting them all at risk. He had to stop this guy and make sure he couldn't hurt anyone that Jason cared about again.

'So, are you going to go to the police?' Nan asked.

Jason wasn't sure. He trusted Detective Riggs but he also knew the best way to deal with this situation was on his own. That way no-one else would get hurt. 'Maybe, Nan. I might see Detective Riggs tomorrow. But I think Richie is going to be pissed off, and he's going to come for me. And when he does, I'll be ready.'

Nan patted his knee. 'I know you will. But for now, I think we should go into the lounge room and sing a few songs. Don't you think?'

Jason laughed. As always, Nan knew exactly what he needed. 'Yeah, Nan. I think that's just what we should do.'

CHAPTER 19

The next morning, Jason woke up early. He dressed and walked down to the beach, enjoying the early morning sunlight and the few early birds who were jogging, swimming and walking dogs. He felt a coiled tension throughout his body. He knew what it was. It was the expectation that Richie would be well and truly pissed off that he'd got out of the trap he'd set in the alley. Not only did Jason escape without getting seriously messed up, but one of Richie's goons had been arrested. The guy would be apoplectic. Jason tried to put himself in Richie's shoes. It was hard trying to understand the mind of someone who was obviously a psychopath, but he could at least try.

Richie was out to get him, and that wasn't going to change. Jason had unknowingly moved in on his turf, and tried to help his daughter, who was obviously living in fear of the goons who worked for her dad. Richie had lost one of his henchmen, but Jason assumed that brawny, brainless thugs for hire weren't that hard to come by. He'd find another expendable guy to work for him. Jason had proved he wasn't that easy to take down, so he guessed Richie's next move would be going after the people he loved. Top of the list of people he cared about were Inny and Jax. They were sensible, cautious kids, but Jason thought he'd better give them a heads-up to be on their guard.

He grabbed a coffee from the van near the beach and pulled out his phone. His kids would be awake. Plus, even if they were sleeping in, this was pretty important. He tried Jax first. The phone rang for what seemed like an eternity before going through to voicemail. He didn't bother leaving a message. Then he tried Inga. Her phone rang out as well. A ripple of apprehension went through him, but he told himself that it was fine. Jax would probably be on the tennis court at this time of the morning, practising his serve or something. And maybe Inga was sleeping in. Or maybe she was just in the shower, or having breakfast, and didn't hear her phone.

Jason thought about Mia. He didn't think Richie would know about her, but just in case he thought he'd better get in touch with her and make sure she was okay. He'd sent her a message the night before, after the confrontation in the alley, to let her know he was okay, but a phone call wouldn't hurt. Plus, he wanted to talk to her.

Mia answered on the first ring. 'Good morning.' Her voice was husky, as though she'd just woken up.

'Good morning, beautiful. I hope I didn't wake you?'

He could hear the warmth in her voice. 'No, you didn't, although I wouldn't mind if you did. I'm just reading the news and drinking coffee in bed.'

'Mmm. Wish I was there with you. Sounds cosy.'

She laughed. 'Yeah, I wish you were here too.' Her voice became more serious. 'But tell me how it went yesterday. Was it a trap?'

Jason laughed. 'Yep. You called it. I met the girl in the alley then got jumped by two big gorillas with a gun.'

Her voice was filled with concern. 'Are you okay? How did you get away from them?'

He laughed again. 'Let's just say they weren't all that smart. It was pretty easy to out-think them. And once I got them to ditch the gun, I used all the dirty fighting tricks I learned from growing up with my brothers. Easy done.'

'Oh, that's good. I'm glad you got away. Still, it was a risk. I was worried about you.'

He decided he liked the idea of a beautiful woman being concerned for his welfare. 'Mmm, well, you don't need to worry about me, Mia.

I'm tougher than I look, you know.' He laughed. Then it was Jason's turn to grow serious. 'The risk paid off, though. I found out Mr White's real identity. Turns out he's a guy called Richard Whitten who I went to school with. He's a drug-dealing psychopath these days, and apparently he's got a grudge against me. Not only that, but I've somehow accidentally moved in on his turf. I'm a bit concerned he might try and get at the people I care about.'

Mia's voice was playful. 'Oh, and that includes me, does it?'

He laughed. 'Yeah, it sure does. I don't know if he even knows about you, but I thought I'd give you a heads-up anyway. Just be careful, please Mia.'

'Okay. I will,' she said softly. 'But please promise me that you'll be careful too.'

'I will,' he promised. 'And as soon as all this is over, I'm really looking forward to spending some more time with you.' He said goodbye, trying not to get distracted by the thought of her in bed. He had to keep his mind clear today. He had a psychopath to deal with.

Half an hour later, he still couldn't get either of the kids on the phone. Trying to calm his rising panic, he dialled his ex-wife's number.

'Good morning, Susan,' he said, when she answered. 'I've been trying to get hold of Inga and Jax. Do you know where they are?'

'Hi, Jason.' In the background he could hear the clank of feed buckets and a horse whinnying – the sounds of the stables where she kept her horses. 'Jax went to the tennis club early this morning, and I think Inga's gone to meet a friend for brunch. Have you tried their phones?'

'Yes, I have.' He tried to keep his voice neutral. 'Neither of them are answering.'

'Well, that's not unusual. They might just be busy, Jason.'

He took a deep breath. 'Right. Do you know which friend Inga is meeting?'

Susan sighed, and he could sense her irritation. 'No. She just said she was meeting a friend. No idea who.'

'Okay. I'm not sure if they've told you anything about what's been going on at work, but I'm just a bit concerned.' He downplayed his worries, not wanting Susan to panic. 'Can you let me know if you hear from them?'

'Yeah, they told me a bit. You do manage to get yourself into some situations, Jason. But sure, I'll let you know if I hear from them.'

'Thanks Susan.' He thought for a moment about telling her to be careful too but decided against it. Susan was pretty tough. If anyone came after her, she'd probably stab them with a hay fork or something. He said goodbye, and hung up.

A few surfers were riding the little waves onto shore. The surf wasn't great today, not much swell, so it was good for those just learning to ride the waves. It was a spectacular morning, but Jason wasn't paying much attention to the scene in front of him. Instead, he was thinking about his next moves. He had to check his kids were okay, that was his highest priority. He could drive to the tennis club and check on Jax, but where would he find Inga? Even if he knew which friend she was meeting, he didn't have any of her friends' phone numbers. He could drive around the cafes he knew she liked, but still, he might not find her. He felt a rising sense of concern. He tried to convince himself it was just a coincidence that they both weren't answering, but it wasn't working. He drained the last of his coffee and started back toward his house. At least he could go to the tennis club and check on Jax. One step at a time.

His phone rang. Jason snatched it out of his pocket and looked at the number. It was Stella. He'd saved her number after she phoned him last time. For an instant, he wondered if she was phoning to lure him into another trap. She was Richie's daughter, after all. She seemed vulnerable and troubled, but maybe she was a psychopath like her father, and just really good at acting. But still, he couldn't imagine what it must be like being his daughter. He felt sorry for her. Either way, Stella might have some information he needed. He answered on the second ring. 'Hello?'

Stella's voice was jagged, as though she was afraid, and she was speaking quietly. Still, he could hear her ragged breaths. 'Hello, Jason?'

'Stella, are you okay?'

'Yes, I'm… I'm fine. But it's your kids.' An icy hand gripped his heart as she spoke. 'I, I think one of the men who works for my dad has them. I overheard Dad talking on the phone.' Her words came out in a jumble amidst her ragged breathing.

Jason's voice was cold and hard. 'He has my kids? Where are they, Stella?'

'I… I don't know,' she stuttered. 'I think he's taking them somewhere. My dad said he's going to go there and meet him. I don't know where.'

'Where's your dad now?'

'He… he just left. He just got a phone call and then left right away. I shouldn't be talking to you, he's got me locked up here, and there's someone who's supposed to be watching me…'

'Stella, think hard. Did you overhear anything else?'

'No. I'm sorry, Jason.' He could tell that she was crying. 'I'm sorry for everything.'

'Hey, Stella, it's not your fault. Please, just stay safe. I'll call you when I can.' He was already running toward his car. 'And Stella, thank you for phoning me.'

Jason hung up and sprinted the rest of the way to his car, ignoring the twinges of pain from his bad knee. This bastard, this absolute fucker, had his kids. If anything happened to them… He couldn't even finish the thought. Nothing would happen to them because he wouldn't allow that. He was going to find this psychopath right now, and finish this.

The only question was, where was he taking them? Of course, Jason knew there could only be one answer to that question. This would finish where it had begun. At his building site. The police had closed it down, so there wouldn't be anyone there. He gunned the car out of the driveway, almost sideswiping a station wagon in the process, and jammed his foot hard on the accelerator. Then he broke almost every road rule in the book to get there. His kids were in trouble, and the roiling rage inside him thundered in his ears. He was going to protect his kids, no matter what.

CHAPTER 20

Jason screeched to a halt outside the building site, his car slewing sideways as he jammed on the brakes. Immediately, he could tell something was amiss. The gate in the security fence was hanging open, although the site was deserted. He paused for a moment, listening intently. The site was eerily still and quiet. Jason could hear his pulse hammering in his ears, but other than that, there were no sounds coming from the site or the buildings nearby.

Jason stepped up to the gate, noticing that the chain securing it had been severed. A pair of heavy-duty bolt cutters lay on the ground just inside the gate. Clearly, Richie had no intention of covering his tracks, which was an ominous sign. Jason stepped inside the security fence, glancing around. There was no sign of movement inside the site. The security camera over the front door was hanging from its wires, smashed and useless. It felt like a little breadcrumb, luring him to follow the trail. Obviously, Richie knew he'd work out where his kids were and hightail it here as fast as he could. He expected Jason to follow his little clues and go charging in through the front door. *Fuck that*, thought Jason. It was all well and good walking into a trap when it was only his safety on the line, but when his kids were in the equation, Jason would rein in every single emotion and exercise perfect caution.

He walked closer to the front door. It was shut but the door jamb was damaged, obviously from a crowbar. That must have been where they got in. He'd put money on the fact that if he charged through that door, one of Richie's goons would be there, waiting to smack him over the head with that crowbar. Instead, he walked quietly around to the back of the building. The rear of the site was cluttered with pallets of bricks, racks of pipes for the plumbing, and extra scaffolding. Jason used his key to open the little garden shed that held tools and supplies, feeling the tension rippling throughout his body. His every instinct told him to kick in the door and burst into the site, taking no prisoners and hauling his kids out of danger. But he had to play it smart. And the first thing he needed was a weapon.

Jason grabbed a nail gun off the shelf by the door and a heavy hammer from another shelf. He'd put the nail gun there himself. He'd caught some of the apprentices playing with it one afternoon. They'd jammed the mechanism that stopped the gun from firing unless it was pressed up against a plank of wood and they were using it to shoot cans across the yard. Jason had been impressed by their ingenuity. In fact, he'd been slightly tempted to join in with the game. The gun wasn't very accurate, but it could shoot a spray of nails 30 metres or so across the yard, skewering the tin cans, but he'd taken it off them anyway. There was no way he wanted Work Safe or his insurance company coming down on him like a tonne of hot bricks.

It would do. He held the nail gun in one hand and slipped the hammer into his belt so he had the other hand free. Leaving the shed open, he walked to the back of the building, listening intently. It was still silent, the only noise coming from the traffic on the busier streets closer to the beach. If they were expecting him at the main front entrance, he'd come in through the rear door. He opened it quietly, thinking hard. The building was three stories high, with two luxury apartments on each floor and a set of shops on the ground floor at the front. That was a lot of area to search. So he had to put himself in Richie's head. He didn't want to try to think like a murderous psychopath, but he had no choice.

Not the ground floor. He'd go somewhere high. Probably the second floor, maybe even the third. And he'd want space. He'd think that he was too good to be crowded into a small space. So the big, open-plan living space in one of the apartments. But which one? He thought for a moment. For all of Richie's craziness, he was practically a hermit, hiding out at the Galaxy as far as Jason could work out. So, chances were, he'd be in the top floor apartment, the one with the view of the Galaxy. Somewhere where he felt comfortable. If he was wrong, Jason ran the risk of getting ambushed as he searched the building. But if he was right, he'd have the element of surprise on his side.

There were two ways to get to the top-floor apartments. There would be three ways, but the elevator was not yet in service. There was the main staircase, which ran up the centre, between the apartments. Then there was the emergency exit stairwell that ran up the back of the building, with exit doors on each floor. Jason was certain Richie would have a goon stationed at the top of the main stairwell, ready to ambush him as soon as he came into view. He'd be a sitting duck if he went up the main stairs. Richie probably knew about the emergency exit as well, and he might have a goon stationed in that stairwell too. But maybe not. Maybe the goon would be stationed on the other side of the exit door, on the third floor.

There was another way to get into the third-floor apartment. It was much riskier, but his kids were worth the risk. Jason stood stock-still for a minute, listening. Maybe he'd been wrong and his kids weren't here. Maybe Richie was holding them at the Galaxy, or somewhere else. He had to be sure they were here, otherwise he'd be wasting time he could be using to find them wherever else they were. Then, in the silence, he caught the faint sound of a voice. It was Inga. He'd know that voice anywhere, even from a distance. The voice that answered her was deep and firm; more of a growl. He couldn't make out the words but guessing from the intonation Inga had been trying to argue, and one of Richie's goons had told her to be quiet.

They were here. The thought sent a rush through him. His pulse was already hammering in his ears, and another burst of adrenaline shot through him. He was grateful for that, because it kept his mind sharp and off the pain in his knee. He had to put his plan into action.

There was no time to waste. He couldn't bear the thought of his kids being frightened or even slightly worried for even a moment, much less the thought of Richie hurting them. If his kids got so much as a scratch on them, Jason would tear the bastard limb from limb.

Keeping to the back of the building, Jason glanced into the foyer to see if he could spot anyone. By the front door, just as he'd suspected, was a dark shadow, standing to one side, perfectly still. One of the goons. Jason slipped carefully away, opening the fire door into the back emergency stairwell, thanking every deity he could think of that the hinges didn't creak. He went up the stairs, grateful for his soft-soled running shoes. His feet didn't make a sound on the bare concrete steps. He continued upwards, past the first- and second-floor doors. At the third-floor door, he stopped and listened for a moment. On cue, there was a muffled cough from the other side of the door. Probably another of Richie's goons. If Jason had to bet, based on the few sounds he'd heard, he'd say that Richie was holding the kids in the east apartment, in the spacious main lounge.

And he *was* betting on that. He continued on up the stairwell to the tiny landing at the top. He took a breath and opened the service entrance to the roof, hoping the hinges wouldn't squeal. Once again, there was no noise. There was a pull-down ladder in the service entrance cavity, and Jason pulled it down and began climbing. The square access door was only just wide enough for him to fit through with his shoulders turned sideways. As soon as his head cleared the roof, he blinked in the bright morning sunlight, then hauled himself onto the roof. It was fairly flat, and strewn with bits of detritus left by the building crew. There were still a few loose wires up here that needed to be secured. Part of the roof had a deck, accessible by the main stairway, but here at the back of the building, the space was filled with air conditioner units and various other bits of functional equipment that didn't need to be inside.

Jason walked right to the edge of the building, protected by a raised ledge all around the roof. Here was the biggest part of his gamble. He was hoping it would pay off and not end with him splattered on the dirt below, but the adrenaline rushing through his system was still driving him, making his heart beat fast and all of his senses feel like they were in overdrive. Jason found the switch on the nail gun and turned it on, making sure the safety catch was still engaged. He went to the ledge and glanced over. Below, he could see the huge floor-to-ceiling windows of the third-floor apartment – or rather, the holes where the windows would soon be installed. For now, they were gaping voids with a layer of thin chipboard across the bottom to stop anyone from accidentally tumbling out.

Jason sent a quick prayer skyward that his knee would hold out and then, in one smooth motion, he grabbed the ledge with his free hand and swung his legs over the top, balancing his torso on the ledge. He pushed himself over, still clinging on to the ledge for a moment. He swung his legs inward as he dropped, and then let go, hoping like hell he'd have enough momentum to get inside the window. He swung in, freefalling for a heart-stopping moment before hitting the concrete floor of the third-floor apartment, just inside the window. One of his feet caught on a plywood panel as he did, knocking it out of the window frame. A jolt of pain rippled up from his knee, and he swung his free arm to get his balance so he didn't fall backward through the gap where the plywood had been. But he was in.

And he had been right. Inside the large open space were the two most precious people in the world to him, Jax and Inga, both staring at him as though he'd grown an extra head. After a moment of frozen silence, they both shouted 'Dad!' and stepped in his direction. He opened his arms, still holding the nail gun in one hand, and moved toward them.

Then a voice from the other side of the room made him pause. 'Stop.' He looked up to see Richie Whitten, or Mr White, or whatever the fuck he was calling himself these days. Little Richie. He had matured and developed fine lines, grey hairs, a receding hairline. A permanent bitter expression. But it was still him. Still the same kid Jason had known since primary school.

Except now, Richie was holding a black pistol in one hand, and he had it pointed directly at Jax and Inga. He spoke, his voice dripping with menace. 'Hello Jason. I've been wondering when you'd get here.'

CHAPTER 21

Jason froze in place, holding the nail gun out to one side. He'd expected Richie to have a gun. He just wasn't sure what to do about it. Yet.

'Jax, Inga,' he said, slowly and carefully. 'Get behind me.'

Richie waved the gun at them. His eyes were bulging and looked slightly bloodshot. It gave him an unhinged look. Chances were he was sampling his own product, whatever the fuck kind of drugs Richie's gang sold out of the Galaxy. His voice was deeper than the kid Jason remembered, but it still had that nasal whine to it. 'Kids, I'd suggest you pay attention to me, not your dad. Unless you want me to shoot him in the head.'

'Hey Richie,' Jason spoke as calmly as he could. 'Come on now. This is just between us. Why don't you let them go? They shouldn't be involved in this.'

Richie laughed, a short, high-pitched, hyena-like sound that instantly brought back memories of Jason's childhood. He could remember Richie's laugh. Had he always sounded so batshit crazy? Why hadn't they realised he was a budding psychopath back then? 'No, Jason. I'm calling the shots around here. And the kids are staying. You can put that tool down, too, whatever it is.'

Of course, Richie didn't recognise a nail gun when he saw one. He'd probably never done a day's physical work in his life. 'Okay, okay,' Jason spoke soothingly, holding the gun out to one side. 'Here I am, look, putting it down.' As he did, he edged sideways, slowly moving his body in front of the kids. 'Hey, man, are you going to tell me what this is all about? I don't get it. Why the graffiti? Why the damage to my site? I'm starting to get the feeling you don't like me, man.' He kept his tone light, as though he was speaking to a cranky toddler. As he spoke, he carefully laid the nail gun on the floor and shuffled sideways some more until he was standing directly in front of Jax and Inga.

'Get away from them,' Richie snapped, tension lacing his voice. Then he shouted, 'Mick! Get in here.'

'Okay, okay,' Jason held his hands up but stayed exactly where he was, shielding his kids. 'Come on man, are you going to tell me what this is all about?'

There were footsteps at the door and one of Richie's goons came in. It was the big guy from the alley, the one who'd left his buddy and fled when the cops turned up. Not that Jason felt sorry for Jerry at all, the guy had it coming to him. But still, Mick was a real asshole. Jason saw the surprise flicker across his face when he saw Jason. He must have been guarding the landing, as Jason had guessed. The look of confusion on his face was almost comical as he tried to work out how Jason had made it into the room. He finally looked at the big open window frame and frowned some more, probably wondering if Jason could fly. He clearly wasn't the brightest guy in the world. He was holding a gun as well. Richie must have a good source of illegal weapons.

'Tie him up,' Richie snapped, gesturing at Jason with the gun. Jason could almost feel the tension radiating off him.

'Uhhh,' Mick glanced around the room, looking for something he could use to tie Jason with. The room was bare, aside from some assorted plumbing pipes stacked along one wall and the big concrete kitchen island bench in the area that would become the kitchen, across the room from them. 'Should I go get some rope, boss?'

Richie sighed with frustration. 'No, you moron. Take your belt off and use that.'

'Right, boss.' Mick ambled across the room toward Jason. 'Put your hands behind your back.'

Jason did as he was told, revolving his body a quarter turn as he did so, so he could see his kids. He raised an eyebrow at them, asking without words if they were ok. Both Inga and Jax nodded at him and smiled. They were tough kids. 'Stay behind me,' Jason said, softly. Then he turned his attention back to Mick.

Mick stepped in front of Jason to get around to where his hands were, and for a moment he was between Jason and Richie. That was his first mistake. His second mistake was that he'd started taking his belt off and was holding his gun by the butt as he did so. As soon as he was within range, Jason spun toward him and punched, aiming for the arm that was holding the gun. He connected, and the jolt knocked the gun out of Mick's loose grasp. It clattered to the floor. Again, the look of surprise flashed across his big, dumb face. 'Fuck,' Mick swore.

The gun was close enough that Jason could reach it with his foot, but what he really wanted was fewer guns in this space. He swung his foot and kicked it, with a perfect, soccer player's aim, so that the menacing black weapon skittered across the floor toward the open window. It reached the edge of the huge, open window space, and teetered on the edge for a second before tipping over and falling to the ground below.

'You moron! You useless imbecile!' Richie berated the man. Seeing the expression on Mick's face as he watched his gun disappear out the window, Jason almost felt sorry for him. But then he reminded himself that Mick was a murderous, violent bastard who had kidnapped Jason's own kids. And he'd probably been the one who killed Frank. He saw red at the thought.

'You fucking prick,' Mick shouted. Then he lunged for Jason. He landed a solid punch to Jason's face, connecting with his jaw. But Jason was quick too, and he stepped in, using Mick's momentum to connect with the man's solar plexus. While Mick gasped for air, Jason landed another hit to Mick's face. He stumbled backward, taking a moment to gather his senses. Then he sucked in a deep breath and charged toward Jason, intent on tackling him. In an instant, Jason remembered what he and his brothers had often done to each other as kids. Their fighting style had been rough and ready, but they'd always had an instinct for how to get each other off balance. At the last moment, just before Mick's bulk slammed into him, Jason dodged to the side. With the barrelling momentum that was supposed to hit Jason, Mick stumbled forward. For a moment Jason thought he'd be able to right himself, but it was too late. Mick windmilled his arms as he fell forward. Right toward the huge open window space. Just like the gun had, he teetered for a second before falling like a stone, right out of the open window space. His shriek was ear-splitting as he fell, then there was a dull thud on the dirt below. Jason looked out at him, lying on the ground, one leg bent at an unnatural angle. Even if he wasn't dead, he wouldn't be getting up any time soon.

'What have you done?' Richie snarled, snapping Jason's attention back to the room. Then he shouted in his reedy voice, 'Wes, Wes, get up here.' Wes was presumably the goon who was guarding the front door, but he was too far out of earshot to hear Richie's shouts. There were no sounds of footsteps on the stairs. But even without his backup, Richie still had a gun and Jason didn't.

'Kids, stay behind me,' he said. 'And stay away from that fucking window.' In his peripheral vision he could see that the two of them were standing close together, obviously shaken.

'I'm going to make you pay for that,' Richie whined. 'You'll be sorry.'

'Yeah?' Jason asked. He knew he had to get Richie talking. 'So why don't you tell me exactly what I'll be sorry for? What have I done to you?'

Richie's eyes were wide and his nostrils flared. His face twitched. 'Don't play innocent with me. You know exactly what you've done.'

Jason was sure he didn't. 'Why don't you spell it out for me anyway.'

Richie was silent for a moment, and then he started talking, bitterness and self-pity lacing his words. 'You have no idea what it was like for me when I was growing up, do you? Being the rich kid in a poor neighbourhood. All you kids wanted to be friends with me, but only so you could get stuff off me. Swim in my pool. Play my Nintendo.'

Oh, boo fucking hoo, thought Jason. *Must have been so hard to come from a rich family.* He held himself back from rolling his eyes. 'What does that have to do with me?'

'All the other kids looked up to you. When they should have been looking up to *me*. I was the natural leader in that place, but instead they followed you around. And you were just a *clown*.' Vitriol was dripping from his voice. 'Still, I wanted to be your friend. I let you swim in my pool, ride my bike, eat the snacks at my house. And how did you repay me? You were friends with the *other* kids.'

'I was friends with you too,' Jason said. He was sure he was remembering that correctly.

'But you should have been friends with *only* me. We could have run that neighbourhood. That school. Instead, you treated me like shit.'

Richie was sounding more and more unhinged. But getting him talking was working. He had lowered the gun and was focusing all of his attention on Jason. In the meantime, Inga and Jax had been sidling across the room, away from the window and the lunatic with the gun. Smart kids, Jason thought. He had to keep Richie talking. 'Right, right. I'm sorry I hurt your feelings, man.'

Richie was barely listening to him. 'It was like that all the way through school. Things that should have been mine, you took. I worked hard to get good grades, and you did fuck all, just clowned around in class, and you got good grades too. And then, when I should have been school captain, the whole damn school acted like you were school captain. You stole it from me.' His voice rose with each word, menace and anger lacing his tone. 'You don't know what it was like to have to sit back and watch that and not to be able to do anything about it.'

'So that's why you chose a life of crime?' Jason asked. He was keeping an eye on his kids, who were by now in the kitchen area. They ducked down behind the concrete island bench. Safe. Thank fuck for that.

Richie let out a short bark of laughter. 'Ha. A life of crime. You don't know anything about my life. The Galaxy is the centre of the biggest drug distribution network in the state. I'm raking in thousands every day. You might have stolen all the respect I deserved in my high school days, but now I'm the most respected, the most feared man in the city. You should be grovelling before me.'

No thanks, Jason thought. 'Where do the drugs come from?' he asked. He couldn't care less, but he thought Riggs would be quite interested.

Richie barked with laughter. 'Wouldn't you like to know? Well, I'll tell you. What's the harm, you're not getting out of here alive, anyway. They come in on the big cruise ships. I've got people on about a dozen ships that bring them in.'

Interesting. Jason filed away the information to tell Riggs. 'Right. Still, Richie, I don't understand. High school was a long time ago. Why go after me now?'

Richie's face twisted with fury. 'You came into the Galaxy about a month ago. Waltzed in like it was nothing, with that friend you chose over me, back in school. And you tried to act like the knight in shining armour, rescuing Stella. My Stella. Yeah, you were right. She is my daughter. And you were going to steal her from me, too.'

Jason thought back to the night he'd first gone to the Galaxy with Pauly. 'I wasn't trying to steal her. I was just stepping in to stop that asshole from threatening her.'

'That asshole was working for me. Keeping her in line. On my orders. And you got in the way. You see why I couldn't let that slide. And then this building project – you were trying to get in on my turf, trying to change this neighbourhood, threatening the empire I'd built. I couldn't have you here. I had to shut this project down and get you away from here before you fucked up everything I'd built. And you didn't take a hint. Never could.' He laughed bitterly.

Jason could see how that one tiny incident might set off someone with such a tenuous grip on reality. He could see how his presence in the area might have felt like a threat. Richie was clearly deranged. And Jason's patience had run out. His kids were safe behind the kitchen island, and he'd had enough of Richie's bitter whining. He'd stopped pointing the gun at Jason, so that was a positive, but he was still holding it, waving it around as he talked. It wasn't quite enough. Jason needed to distract him for just a moment.

And at that moment, he caught a glimpse of Jax out of his peripheral vision. Apparently reading his mind, Jax reached out from behind the bench and shoved a stack of plumbing pipes leaning up against the wall. They fell over with a terrific crash, causing Richie to jump with surprise and turn in the direction of the noise.

It was just enough. Jason bent and scooped up the nail gun from the floor, clicked off the safety catch, and aimed. And then he prayed like hell his aim would be true. He jammed his finger on the trigger just as Richie realised what was happening and swung back to aim the gun at him. Jason fired a stream of nails at him, and one of them lodged in Richie's gun arm. He screamed and dropped the gun. That was all Jason needed.

CHAPTER 22

n an instant, Jason ran. His powerful strides hit the floor, toward the gun lying at Richie's feet. He put everything he had into it. Richie's eyes bulged as he looked first at the nails lodged in his arm and then at Jason, barrelling across the room toward him. Jason's knee spasmed with pain, but he ignored it, focusing everything on getting to the gun before Richie could reach down and pick it up.

Richie bent over, grabbing the barrel just as Jason reached him, hitting him with the full force of his momentum. Richie screamed again as he fell backward, but he kept his hold on the gun. Jason grabbed it too, trying to wrestle it from his grip. At the same moment, Jason heard the rhythmic slaps of footsteps running up the concrete staircase. The goon downstairs must have finally heard Richie scream, or realised something wasn't right. Then Jason heard another sound – probably what had made the goon run. It was a police siren in the distance, getting closer.

The weight of Jason's body was pressing down on Richie's torso, stopping him from getting up as Jason tried to pull the gun away from him. But Richie was unnaturally strong –possibly from drugs in his system, or maybe just pure desperation. For an instant, he almost managed to get his finger on the trigger of the gun. The footsteps outside the door were getting closer, meaning another asshole with a gun was about to burst in. Jason thought of his kids sheltering behind the bench in the kitchen area. There was no way he was going to let anything happen to them. Despite the awkward angle, despite Richie's wiry strength, he wrapped his hand around the barrel of the gun and pulled. Richie yelped as he lost his grip on the weapon. Then, in one swift movement, Jason pushed himself upright and pulled Richie up to standing too. He flipped the gun around in his hand and trained it on Richie. 'Don't fucking move,' he growled.

The footsteps approached the doorway, slowing, and Jason ran through a dozen calculations in his head. The goon would be able to see from the doorway where his kids were hiding, and even though he now held a gun in his hand, he couldn't allow them to be in danger. But he didn't want to shoot anyone – not even one of Richie's murderous thugs. He transferred the gun to his left hand and pulled the hammer from his belt with his right. He lifted it over his shoulder, and as the man dressed in black burst through the doorway with a gun in his hand, Jason let fly. The hammer spiralled through the air and hit him in the side of his balaclava-covered head. He grunted with pain and staggered backward, the gun falling from his hand.

'Jax, now! Get the gun,' shouted Jason, and his son, already coiled and ready to spring, darted from behind the bench. He bolted toward the gun, reaching it before the goon had even stopped staggering. Then he held it in two hands, pointing it directly at the bigger man. The big man could see when he was defeated and slumped to the floor, holding one hand to the side of his head. Jason figured he'd have a pretty big headache for the rest of the day.

'You bastard! You asshole!' Richie swore. Now that he'd let go of the hammer, Jason grabbed Richie by the shoulder, still training the gun at his head. The distant sound of police sirens was getting louder and louder.

'Yeah, well at least I'm not a murderous psychopath,' Jason said. 'You're going to prison. For all the things you did to me, and for all the drug trafficking, but most of all, for killing Frank. He was my friend, and you're going to rot in jail for what you did to him.'

Richie laughed, a maniacal sound. The sound echoed in the big room. 'They'll never get me. Not for that. Not for any of it. I've got an airtight alibi. And, as for today, you lured me over here so you could torture me and kill off one of my bodyguards. That gun's got your fingerprints on it. And it's my story against yours. Wes here will back me up. You should've shot him while you had a chance, he'll say anything I tell him to. And I've got the best lawyers that money can buy – I'm never going to see jail, you can count on that.'

'I wouldn't be so sure of that,' Inga said, coming out from behind the kitchen bench. Jax was still standing, the gun pointing at the guy on the floor. Inny walked across the room, holding a phone screen so Jason and Richie could see it, albeit from a safe distance. She pressed play, and a video began. It had obviously been taken from behind the kitchen bench, with Inga holding the phone at the very corner. But Richie's face was visible. His voice rang out from the little screen. *The Galaxy is the centre of the biggest drug distribution network in the state. I'm raking in thousands every day. You might have stolen all the respect I deserved in my high school days, but now I'm the most respected, the most feared man in the city. You should be before me.*

Jason grinned. 'Oh my god, Inga, well done. I think the cops will be pretty interested in seeing that little video.'

Richie let out a shriek and lunged toward Inga, trying to grab the phone out of her hand. But Jason was ready for him. He yanked on Richie's arm, pulling him backward and jerking his arm up behind his back. It was the same arm that still had a couple of nails lodged in it, and Richie yelped with pain. 'You're not going anywhere near my daughter,' Jason growled.

The police sirens came to a crescendo, and a squeal of tyres outside the building announced they'd arrived.

'I wonder how they knew we were here?' Jason asked.

'Oh, that was me, too,' Inny said. 'I called them when we were hiding behind that bench over there. Well, I couldn't really talk, so I texted my friend and she called them.'

Jason laughed. 'Oh my god. You kids are incredible. You just did everything so perfectly. Jax pushing over those pipes to distract him at just the right time, and Inga, I can't believe you managed to video his little monologue. You guys are truly amazing.'

'You did pretty good as well, Dad. I couldn't believe it when you came in through that window,' Jax said.

'Fell in through the window, you mean,' Inga teased.

Jason laughed. 'I just can't believe these dumb asses didn't take your phone off you.'

'Oh, they tried,' Inga said. 'They took Jax's phone, and they searched my pockets, but they didn't do a very good job of it.' She patted an almost hidden pocket on the leg of her pants. 'I've been hiding my phone from you and Mum for years,' she laughed. 'Turns out I'm pretty good at it.'

A faint voice from one of the lower floors drifted up to them. 'This is the police. You need to come out with your hands up.'

Jason nodded toward the door. 'Come on. We'd better go before they storm the place. We don't want to get through all of this just to get taken down by the police. Stay behind me kids.'

He jerked Richie's arm, pushing him forward. Then he walked out of the apartment toward the staircase, shouting, 'Riggs, it's me. We're all okay, and we're coming out. Don't shoot.' He walked out onto the landing, still twisting Richie's arm up behind his back and pushing him along in front of him. 'Come on Richie. I think my friend Detective Riggs is going to be very happy to meet you.'

EPILOGUE

The restaurant had a view of the ocean. It was a still, beautiful evening. The lights from the city were reflected in the water, giving the impression there was another one floating just under the surface. Jason looked around. He was sitting on a wide deck at a table that could seat a crowd. And tonight, he was expecting a crowd.

One of the first to arrive was Mia. She wore a soft black dress that clung to her curves; she looked stunning, as usual. Jason stood to kiss her and felt the same thrill of attraction as when he'd first met her. They'd been dating for, well, around six months now. They were both busy people, so it was a slow progression, but Jason loved the time they spent together.

Then Jax and Inga came over, each giving him a big hug. They'd been even closer since the day at the building site when Richie had held them hostage. Every time Jason saw them, he felt an enormous wave of gratitude to the universe that they were safe and apparently unscathed by the experience.

Rachel was here as well, in her usual impeccably tailored outfit. She was such an elegant woman, but didn't seem to mind when Jason swept her up in a big bear hug. He didn't know where he'd be without her. Probably impossibly tangled in some ill-advised venture, or up to his eyeballs in account books that he honestly didn't care about. He was grateful for her steady, reassuring presence in his life.

Pauly was next to arrive, with his wife and family in tow. Then a few of Jason's other mates, some of them with their families as well. They had to pull a couple more chairs over so everyone could fit around the table.

A few people Jason had wished could be there weren't able to come, but on a night like this, he could still feel their presence and well wishes from afar. He'd been to see his mum and dad earlier that day, and his brothers had sent congratulatory texts. And, of course, before he came to the restaurant he'd been to Nan Dooksie's house, taking her a home-cooked meal and a big slab of carrot cake. He'd invited her to come to the restaurant but she'd said in her firm, no-nonsense tone that she was planning on watching her shows on TV and then going to bed early. But she'd also given him a big hug and told him she was proud of him, so that was enough.

Once the waiter had delivered a round of drinks, Jason raised his glass. 'I just wanted to say thank you all for your support and encouragement over the last few months. It's been a hard slog, but the apartments are finished! Cheers everyone.'

There was a chorus of cheers and congratulations from around the table, and everyone clinked glasses and drank. Jason felt another wave of gratitude. The project had been a marathon, but they'd passed the final round of compliance checks today, and that was worth celebrating. The rest of the work was cosmetic – landscaping, furnishing the display apartment and clearing away all the building detritus.

'There's something else to celebrate, isn't there?' Mia prompted him. There was a chorus of teasing around the table, all wondering if he and Mia were engaged. But neither of them had time for that.

'That's right,' Jason said. 'I got a call from Detective Riggs today. Richie was sentenced to twenty years in jail for Frank's murder today. He didn't do it himself, of course, but he gave the instruction to one of his men. He's also facing separate charges for kidnapping Jax and Inga and, of course, there were the charges related to his drug distribution ring.'

That whole case was going to take a bit longer to unravel, but Richie would certainly see some jail time for that as well. The guy was going to be rotting in prison, even with his expensive lawyers.

The news got another round of cheers from the table. Jason leaned back in his chair, enjoying the company of his friends. 'Detective Riggs told me something interesting today,' he told Mia. 'The Galaxy is going to be confiscated under proceeds of crime laws. Which means it will be up for sale soon.'

Mia raised her eyebrows at him. 'Are you thinking it would make a good project?'

Jason laughed. Was he that transparent? 'Yeah, that's exactly what I was thinking.' He paused. 'If, of course, Rachel thinks it's a good idea.'

Rachel gave him her trademark stern look, the one that would make anyone who didn't know her as well as Jason did quiver in their seat. Then she smiled. 'I think you've got room for another project in your schedule Jason, now that this one is finished.'

He grinned. 'It's such a great building. Don't you think it would make a great restaurant?'

'Or a great gym,' Jax added.

'A gym with a health food store,' Inga said. 'I could run it for you.'

Jason laughed. 'Yes! I love all those ideas. As soon as Riggs gives us the go-ahead, let's go check it out, shall we?'

Inga looked thoughtful. 'What happened to the girl, Dad? Richie's daughter?'

'Stella? She's actually doing pretty well,' Jason said. 'She's living with her mum now. Turns out she really wants to study graphic design at TAFE, so I've given her a bit of a hand with the fees. I mean, it's only fair, really, seeing as her dad got put in jail because of me,' he joked.

Mia rolled her eyes. 'Not because of you. Because of his own stupidity and criminal activity.'

'Yeah, of course, you're right. But that's not Stella's fault. She deserves a bit of a break.'

Jason also thought about Sandra, Frank's widow. The house she was living in had been a rental, so Jason decided she needed a break as well. He'd set her up in one of the apartments in the new complex. She was moving in on the weekend. With the new shops opening up on the lower level, she'd be able to find a job there as well. It was the least he could do for his mate Frank.

The evening progressed the same way it had started, full of good cheer and plenty of happy conversations. Jason sat back, soaking it all in. The building project, as well as Richie's interference, had taken up so much of his attention for so long it was nice to just be able to enjoy what he had. And he was also excited about the future. The Galaxy would be a great project, there were so many things he could do with that place. Plus, there were lots of other possibilities for other projects, too. He glanced around at the people surrounding him, his friends and family, the people he cared about most. There was so much to be grateful for. And so much still to come...